Lee O. Harris

Interludes

Lee O. Harris

Interludes

ISBN/EAN: 9783337343040

Printed in Europe, USA, Canada, Australia, Japan

Cover: Foto ©Andreas Hilbeck / pixelio.de

More available books at **www.hansebooks.com**

INTERLUDES

SUNG BETWEEN THE ACTS IN THE DRAMA OF TOIL

BY

LEE O. HARRIS

INDIANAPOLIS
CARLON & HOLLENBECK, PRINTERS
1893

Though this be but an humble thing
  To offer at the Muses' shrine,
Pray let your kindness give it grace,
That it may fill some vacant place,
  Among the wreaths you twine.

And though its bloom may not endure,
  I will not mourn its swift decay,
If in your garlands I can set
One sprig of friendship's mignonette
  To blossom for a day.

(iii)

CONTENTS.

(v)

Songs of Nature.

(1)

If thou art one who lovest not to hold
    Communion with the things of field and wood;
Finding no riches in the caltha's gold,
    Nor treasures on the hill nor by the flood;
If in the forest thou hast never stood
    To hear the great fond heart of Nature beat,
Nor felt an impulse in the solitude
    To cast thyself in homage at her feet—
Then go no further, friend, our journey is complete.

But if there dwell an echo in thy heart
    For song of bird or laugh of water-fall;
If from the throng thou fain wouldst steal apart,
    And find thy peace where Nature's voices call;
Then art thou comrade for my journey.   All
    The gold that misers dream of could not buy
Such wealth of wide domain, nor castle hall
    So richly tapestried, as thou and I
Shall find, my friend, with none our entrance to deny.

If thou hast sickened of the dizzy whirl
  Of Mammon's ceaseless treadmill; if thy soul
Is gaining kinship with the ignoble churl
  Who scorns the lark and grovels with the mole;
If from thy shops the smoky shadows roll
  Between thy peace and heaven—then fly the mart,
And let the hand of Nature make thee whole;
  And all thy spirit's wounds will cease to smart,
When she shall pour the oil of gladness on thy heart.

It needs no rush of steam, no clash of wheels
  Through dusty leagues; no toil to mountain height;
No loud Niagara, where the sick sense reels,
  Stunned by the roar and drunken with the sight.
For he who reads the heart of Nature right
  Shall find the vales and hills of home-land sweet.
No fields by day, no starry depths by night,
  Has Heaven vouchsafed, with rapture more complete,
Nor beauty more than this that leans against thy feet.

ALONG THE BANKS OF BRANDYWINE.

THERE is a stream whose emerald shores
    Lie wrapped in Nature's primal shades;
High-canopied with sycamores,
    And set with maple colonnades;
There willows wave their silver plumes,
    And rushes to the breeze incline,
And Summer sows a thousand blooms
    Along the banks of Brandywine.

It has no tale of love and wrong
    To win from pity's eye a tear;
Nor classic story, told in song,
    To bid the pilgrim journey here;
But Nature, to her lover's eyes,
    Displays her beauties, all untamed,
As in her natal paradise
    She walked, unclothed and unashamed.

There Spring, while yet the fields are bare,
    And leafless are the upland bowers,
Unbinds her wealth of golden hair,
    And twines her beauteous brow with flowers;

(5)

While with low-whispered melodies
　She bids the sleeping calthas shine,
And wakes her first anemones
　Along the banks of Brandywine.

And by the pathway where she treads,
　The yellow buttercups arise ;
The fair spring-beauties nod their heads ;
　The violets ope their azure eyes ;
And red-buds, flushing like the morn,
　Beneath her earliest kisses glow,
And nesting robins, from the thorn,
　Shake down a shower of fragrant snow.

But, oh ! when Summer, clothed with grace
　Exceeding all that poets dream,
Stands smiling at her glowing face
　Reflected from the limpid stream,
The vale is clothed anew with bloom
　Of cardinal and columbine,
And winds grow languid with perfume
　Along the banks of Brandywine.

Then all the minstrel bards of June
　Sing melodies, so sweet and low,
That willow-harps are set atune,
　And honeysuckle trumpets blow :

While leafy cymbals of the trees
    Beat out a cadence like a sigh,
And wings of pollen-laden bees
    Make drowsy music as they fly;

Till cooling shadows lay their hands
    Upon the heated brow of day,
And gather up the gleaming strands
    Of sunlight, strewn along the way;
Then where the softest mosses creep,
    And fairest virgin-bowers twine,
Voluptuous Summer lies asleep,
    Along the banks of Brandywine.

Nor is the beauty less complete
    When Autumn comes, serene and fair,
With crimson sandals on her feet,
    And golden-rods among her hair;
Her face aglow with conscious pride,
    As one whose promise can not fail;
Her bounteous palms extended wide,
    To scatter wealth along the vale.

Ah! then the dews by Summer brought,
    To bathe the green of wood and dell,
Grow ruddy as the vintage wrought
    By Cana's sacred miracle;

And wash the maple leaves with red,
  And splash their crimson on the vine,
Among the gold by Autumn spread
  Along the banks of Brandywine.

And when the fires of Autumn burn
  The Summer's bloom to ash of snow,
And from the stream the heart can learn
  A song that prisoned spirits know,
A wealth of beauty still is found;
  A countless store of sparkling gems,
When all the kingly trees are crowned
  With Winter's crystal diadems.

What worldly care hath sting or smart
  For him who wanders here alone,
And feels the pulse of Nature's heart,
  Responsive beat against his own?
Be Melancholy ne'er so sad,
  Her heart to joy must here incline :
And Sorrow's self may well be glad
  Along the banks of Brandywine.

1893.

JUNE.

SWEET May, upon her flowery bier,
　Lies pallid now, her scepter gone,
And June, the queen of all the year,
　Has put her crown of roses on ;
And round her lovely form she twines
A zone of honeysuckle vines.

Bright butterflies and beauteous things
　About her sunny tresses play ;
The humming-bird, on trembling wings,
　With rapture meets her on the way,
And, drinking kisses from her lips,
Grows drunken with the sweets he sips.

The air is heavy with perfume,
　Where, underneath the locust trees,
Or ankle-deep in clover bloom,
　She walks, surrounded by her bees,
While winds that follow in her train
Go sporting through the ripening grain.

She scatters blossoms, wild and sweet,
   With lavish hand along the lanes ;
And by the brook her rosy feet
   Grow redder with the berry stains.
And buttercups, to see her pass,
Stand tiptoe in the meadow grass.

She stoops in tenderness to set
   Her blossoms on the tomb of May,
And plants the fragrant mignonette
   To hide the hyacinth's decay :
And hangs the morning-glory vine
With flagon-cups of dewy wine.

The roses breathe a fragrant sigh
   Where their sweet peony sisters fell ;
The languid poppy blossoms lie
   Asleep on beds of asphodel ;
And birds, too full of joy to sing,
Sit, nestling, where the jasmines cling.

And love-lies-bleeding on the spot
   Where early daisies wooed the bees ;
And, sad, the pale forget-me-not
   Bends o'er the dead anemones ;
And fair verbenas twine and cling
Where crocus blossoms met the spring.

Above the faded daffodils,
　Where lilacs shed their tears of bloom,
The lily's swinging censer spills
　A dewy incense on their tomb,
Till portulacas cease to weep
And fold their rosy hands in sleep.

And Arathusa, by the brook,
　Has put her royal purple on,
And stands, a queen, where Caltha shook
　Her golden tresses in the sun ;
And willows all their harps attune
In songs of welcome to the June.

And I bow down before her feet,
　As pilgrim at some holy shrine :
I drink her breath with roses sweet
　As bacchanalians drink of wine,
Till round my heart such raptures throng
That all my soul goes out in song.

1877.

MOONLIGHT IN THE FOREST.

I STAND where late I heard the twilight winds
　　Go breathing softly through the darkening wood :
They fanned the leaves asleep and stooped to kiss
The nodding flowers good-night, and to the birds
They sang a lullaby, then stole away,
Silently, lightly, as a mother steals
On tiptoe from the cradle of her babe ;
Silence and sleep on shrub, and flower, and tree—
Beat low, my heart, lest thou shouldst break the spell.
And mar the rapture of this sweet repose.
Leap out, my soul, and bathe thee in the waves
Of silvery light, down through the branches poured,
Till o'er the ground a thousand rivulets flow.
And wind among the trees their shining way,
Or flood the pathway with a dew-bright tide,
Save where the silent shadows steal across
And leave their dusky trails upon the grass.
Oh, fair enchanted land wherein I stand,
'Mid gardens richer fruited far than e'er
　　Aladdin found within the wizard's cave !
A mightier power than slave of lamp or ring

Hath waved her wand above the dewy wood,
And lo! a realm of beauty far beyond
The wildest fantasies that Eastern bard
Hath ever wrought from his voluptuous dreams.

Behold! these winding avenues of trees,
Where every bending bough is fruited full
With gold and sparkling gems! where every shrub
Bears diamond bloom, and buds of amethyst
On emerald spray! dim-lighted aisles that lead
Through over-arching vines to jeweled gates,
That ope to courts and palaces as grand
As e'er in Bagdad's days of golden prime
Along the Tigris reared their gilded spires.

Here curtains, woven of the gossamer,
Are hung like veils of silver braid to close
The way that leads to many a lovely bower,
As fair as ever gemmed the fragrant vales
Of Elburz mountains, where Circassian girls
Breathe forth to Persia's odor-laden air
The plaintive strains that tell their captive fate—
That trembling sound! was it a lute's low tone?
Nay, 'twas a zephyr dreaming of the day,
And, half awakened, sighing in its sleep.

Oh, beauteous realm! Fain would I linger here
And sweetly dream through all the summer night.
Alas! too soon the envious clouds have pressed,
With jealous frowns, to intercept the moon—
To steal her light to gild their somber wings
And with the fair magician flies the spell.
The shadows o'er the jeweled aisles expand,
And bower, and court, and gilded palace blend
Into a hueless mass of dusky wood :
The waking winds come moaning down the vale ;
The leaves are all ashiver in the gloom :
So fades the scene—and so our castles fall.

1879.

CLOVER BLOOM.

THE rose inspires the poet's song,
    And interwoven with his bays
Its opening buds might well belong,
    Since he so sweetly sings its praise.
The poppy has its chosen bard ;
    The daisy and the daffodil ;
The violet, on the upland sward ;
    The lily, by the meadow rill.

But who of all the tuneful throng
    That sing of beauty and perfume,
Has deigned to hallow with a song
    Our Western fields of clover bloom ?
Yet here are gracefully combined
    The daisy's worth, the poppy's hue ;
And rivals here the rose may find
    In splendor and in fragrance, too.

Oh, could I wake the voice of song
    That set the echoes all atune,
And poured in witching tones along
    "The Banks and Braes o' Bonny Doon,"

I would not chant, like Scotia's bard,
  Of hawthorn bud, nor tangled broom,
Nor heather on the highland sward,
  But I would sing the clover bloom.

Could I but wield the graceful power
  That won the Ettrick Shepherd's fame,
And still endears that witching hour,
  "The gloaming, when the kye come hame;"
My song should tell of winds that blow
  O'er fields of blossom and perfume,
And raptured bees that, singing, go
  Among the fragrant clover bloom.

Were mine each thrilling tone and word
  Of Erin's bard, whose art has set
Her harp and heart in such accord
  They pulse and throb together yet,
With strains of sweetest melody
  His glowing fancies should be blent,
And woven into song should be
  The shamrock of the Occident.

1878.

SUNSET BEHIND THE CLOUDS.

THE power that paints this glorious scene
   Is but the sun that sinks to rest ;
Those are but clouds that intervene,
Like gold-fringed tapestry, between
   The glowing portals of the west.

And yet, in fancy, I behold
   The shores of some mysterious land,
Through opening curtains that unfold
On beryl walls with gates of gold
   That round a shining city stand.

Yon cloud a mountain seems to rise
   With beetling crags and fissures wide ;
Its summit piercing through the skies
Till all the hues of Paradise
   Come pouring down its glowing side. .

And just below a valley sleeps,
   Encircled by the mountain walls ;
And there a rushing torrent sweeps
Down cloud-wrought hills, and, foaming, leaps,
   In rainbow-tinted water-falls.

And yonder, in the golden light,
  A sunlit ocean ebbs and flows ;
A vessel with its pennon bright,
With crimson hull and sails of white,
  Across the roseate water goes.

But as I gaze the shadows blend,
  And fold about each glowing hue,
Like filmy curtains that descend
To crown some pageant's glorious end
  With one last, grand, dissolving view.

The mountain, of its splendor shorn,
  Stands frowning on a sunless plain ;
The white-winged vessel, tempest-worn,
With canvas rent and pennon torn,
  Lies wrecked upon a leaden main.

Are those the lightning's gleams that run
  Along the cloud-built city's walls?
That thunder— 'tis their evening gun,
 Saluting the departing sun—
  And so the shadowy curtain falls.

1878.

A SUMMER NIGHT.

THE day's departing aureole
  Blends into films of amber light,
That down the sky like vapor roll,
  Fanned westward by the wings of night,
As, flying over field and town,
She lets her dusky tresses down.

Along the hedge the fire-flies glow,
  O'er clinging vine and creeping brier :
And thorns, that blossomed white as snow,
  Are clothed to-night with blooms of fire,
That float on every passing breeze,
And drift like sparks among the trees.

A murmuring sound is faintly borne—
  A tinkling as of fairy feet,
From fields of yellow-tasseled corn,
  Where night-wind minstrels love to meet,
And pipe melodious serenades
Among the ranks of dancing blades.

Oh, hour of peace and pure delight!
   My thoughts are with the winds at play;
As with the minstrels of the night
   I fain would sing my cares away,
My heart, so lately sorrow-worn,
Leaps up to join the dancing corn.
  1877.

THE WOOING OF THE WIND.

THE Wind came through the woods a-wooing,
    Softly sighing as he flew ;
Now, alas ! the flowers are ruing
    All his promises untrue.
    "Violet, with eyes of blue,"
Thus he whispered, gently bending,
"Loving lives have blissful ending !
    Let me live and die with you."

Thus he whispered, sweetly, clearly,
    Vowing he would never stray,
Till the violet loved him dearly—
    Then he laughed and flew away.
    "Slighted love hath bitter ending ! "
Sighed the violet in her pain ;
And, her modest head low bending,
    Never dared look up again.

Then the Wind, his vow forgetting,
    Like a rover, wandered free ;
Thought not once of love's regretting ;
    Recked not of his perfidy.

THE WOOING OF THE WIND.

"Anemone! Anemone!"
Sang he then his song of wooing—
"Loveless hearts are ever ruing!
    Yield yourself to love and me."

Ah! she listened to the rover,
    Thrilling with her promised bliss,
And, like maiden to her lover,
    Tiptoed up to meet his kiss.
Vows, alas! were vain to bind him,
    Trusting one, to love and thee.
On he flew and left behind him
    But a dead anemone.

Now along the brook he lingers,
    Where the golden cowslips gleam;
Where the willows dip their fingers,
    Toying with the laughing stream.
"Caltha, love is all supreme!"
Sighed the truant softly, singing:
"Mateless spirits are but clinging
    To the heaven of a dream."

"Fairest of the spring's fair daughters!"
    Thus the cruel flatterer said:
And her tresses swept the waters,
    As she bent her lovely head,

But he left her there repining,
  Weeping for his broken vow,
And a trace of tears is shining
  On her golden lashes now.

To the wild rose in the thicket
  Flew the rover, false and bold;
And the merry-hearted cricket
  Laughed to hear the tale he told.
"Here a worshiper behold!
Rarest, fairest queen of flowers;
Fit to rule in Flora's bowers;
  Worthy of your crown of gold."

Then this most untrue of rovers
  Stooped to kiss her glowing face;
And the bees, her earliest lovers,
  Left her to his false embrace.
Cruel Wind! his song was tender,
  But he rent her crown apart,
And he left of all her splendor
  Nothing but a bleeding heart.

With the buttercups to dally,
  Flew the wooer, fickle, frail.
And the lily of the valley
  Listened to his heartless tale.

Sweet forget-me-nots grew pale
While they waited his returning.
In her crimson shame stood burning
　Cardinalis of the vale.

Clematis, no longer clinging,
　Yielded wholly to his will;
And he set the blue-bells ringing,
　As he swept along the hill;
But when night came, slowly creeping
　Through the wood, the Wind was gone;
And the flowers all were weeping
　When they wakened at the dawn.

1878.

DAWN AND TWILIGHT.

I SAW the Night a moment stand,
  Expectant and athrill,
While in the east a rosy hand
  Reached, beckoning, o'er the hill.
And then I saw the Morn arise,
  Like Venus from a sea of mist,
And blushes reddened all the skies,
  When Night and Morning kissed.

I saw the Day, aweary, lean
  Against the western hills,
An exile who, with stricken mien,
  His destiny fulfills.
And then I saw a somber flood
  Of darkness wash the light away,
And all the sky grew red as blood,
  Where broke the heart of Day.

1886.

SHADOWS.

A S, where her sleeping infant lies,
   The mother steals, with silent tread,
To shut the sunlight from its eyes,
   And close the curtains round its bed ;
So Night, fond guardian of our rest,
   With noiseless footstep gently goes
To drop the curtains of the west
   Upon a weary world's repose.

On listless wings the winds go by,
   And softly hum a drowsy tune,
Like tired bees that homeward fly,
   O'erfreighted with the sweets of June ;
And shadows, sifting from above,
   Drift slowly o'er the grassy lea,
And seem to sink, and rise, and move,
   Like waves upon a twilight sea.

Like banners o'er a parapet,
   They float above the garden wall ;
On beds of fragrant mignonette,
   Like dusky swarms of bees they fall:

SHADOWS.

They nestle where the jasmine clings,
  And weary, fainting with perfume,
They fold their odor-laden wings,
  And sleep among the poppies' bloom.

Above the pansy beds they rest,
  They fill the lily's cups of gold;
And roses, by the winds caressed,
  Conceal their blushes where they fold;
Among the daffodils they lie;
  They hang upon the flowering thorn;
Like giant birds of night they fly
  Across the fields of waving corn.

Like curtains trailing from the sky,
  Along the vale they fold and sweep;
And in the forest where they lie,
  The night-winds rock the leaves asleep,
Where, thrilling still with day's delight,
  The birds sleep, swinging on the limbs,
And weave in dreams, through all the night,
  The music of their morning hymns.

Along the meadow brook they spread;
  The rushes nod beside the stream;
The poppy hangs her sleepy head,
  And all the drowsy willows dream.

My senses feel their soft caress,
  And thoughts that will no more obey,
On wings outspread and motionless,
  Among the shadows glide away.
1878.

AUTUMN.

THE glowing Summer spread her wings,
    And southward with the robins flew ;
A thousand sweet, familiar things,
    That missed her presence, vanished too.
The blackbirds sang their parting strain,
    And sailed away across the wood,
And Echo, listening long in vain,
    Sank voiceless in the solitude.

The summer winds from field and wold,
    Fled down the glens with many a sigh,
And Summer's sheen of molten gold
    Rolled southward down the paling sky.
And now, brown Autumn hurries past :
    Above the wood her garments trail,
And shadows from her wings are cast
    In dusky hues along the vale.

She spreads a thousand brilliant dyes
    To flush the landscape, far and near,
And, glancing backward as she flies,
    With glory crowns the dying year.

She sweeps across the yellowing fields,
　　She paints the wooded hills with brown;
The elms their leafy offerings yield;
　　The nut-trees fling their tributes down.

The glowing wood, whose summer leaves
　　A hundred mornings bathed in dew,
That from a hundred summer eves
　　Caught every glorious sunset hue,
Now wears Aurora's crown of gold,
　　And Vesper's robe of crimson dye,
And all the colors manifold
　　That flush along the autumn sky.

The oaks in purple masses grow,
　　And flame-like beeches rise between,
And bright-hued maple branches glow,
　　Like crimson stains among the green.
Red lindens on the river shores
　　Stand mirrored where the waters glide,
. And yellow ranks of sycamores
　　Fling golden shallops on the tide.

The bending orchards seem to wear
　　A wealth of colors lately won—
The blush of Summer's rosy air,
　　The gold of Autumn's glowing sun,

The flush that crowns the brow of Spring,
    The russet of the year's decline,
And all the hues the seasons bring
    As offerings to Pomona's shrine.

The meadows, late of verdure shorn,
    Put on a somber robe of gray ;
And field on field of yellow corn
    In purple distance blends away,
To where the hills stand, dim and pale,
    Like spectral watchers by the streams,
And silvery mists above the vale
    Seem hanging o'er a land of dreams.

Oh, Autumn, evening of the year—
    Sweet twilight of a burning day—
Where Summer's glories disappear,
    How bright thy golden splendors play!
And thus, when manhood's summer strife
    Is mellowed into autumn's bloom,
How crowned with bliss the waning life
    Whose sunset glories gild the tomb!
1878.

THE BONNY BROWN QUAIL.

THE song, the song of the bonny brown quail !
　My heart leaps up at the joyous sound,
When first the gleam of the morning pale
　Steals slowly over the dewy ground ;
Ere yet the maples along the hill
　Are draped with fringes of sunlight gold,
I hear the notes of his piping shrill,
　From hill, and valley, and field, and wold—
　　　" 'Tis light ! 'Tis light !
　　　Bob White ! Bob White ! "
Then up he springs to the topmost rail,
　And struts and sings in his proud delight,
The song of the bonny brown quail.

Thus all day long in the tasseled corn,
　And where the willowy waters flow,
In fields by the blade of the reaper shorn ;
　In copse, and dingle, and vale below ;
Where star-crowned asters delight to stand,
　And golden-rods, in their robes of state ;
And in the furrows of fallow-land,
　He calls aloud to his dusky mate :

"All right! All right!
Bob White! Bob White!"
And from her nook where the brambles trail,
    She guides the course of her whirring flight
By the song of the bonny brown quail.

O, bonny bird, with the necklaced throat;
    The song you sing is but brief and shrill,
And yet methinks there never was note
    More sweetly tuned by a master's skill.
And like the song of a vanished day,
    It fills my heart with a subtle joy,
Till, all forgetting my locks of gray,
    I mock your whistle, again a boy.
        "You're right! You're right!
        Bob White! Bob White!"
The hair may whiten, the cheek may pale;
    Time only mellows the old delight
In the song of the bonny brown quail.

When, gliding slowly from east to west,
    The long black shadows begin to crawl;
Ere dew has wetted his speckled breast,
    The brown quail whistles his loud recall:

"Come home! Come home! The wind is still;
  The light is paling along the sky;
The maples are nodding below the hill:
  The world is sleepy and so am I.
      Good-night! Good-night!
      Bob White! Bob White!"
The stars keep watch when the sunbeams fail,
  And morn will waken the golden light,
And the song of the bonny brown quail.

A whirr of wings o'er the stubble brown;
  A patter of feet below the hill:
A close brown circle, all nestled down -
  "Bob White! Good-night!" and all is still.
The rabbit passes with velvet tread,
  And eyes of wonder that wink and peep;
The winds sing lullaby overhead,
  And put the bonny brown quail to sleep.
      Good-night! Good-night!
      Bob White! Bob White!
Would I could hide in the dewy vale,
  And bid the cares of the world good-night,
In song, like the bonny brown quail.
1883.

THE WIND AND THE VIOLET.

[Written for a Child.]

" I HAVE come across the meadows ;
    I have roamed beside the rill ;
I have searched the forest shadows ;
    I have swept along the hill ;
I have crept among the hollows ;
    I have flown across the plain ;
But I find, in wood nor fallows,
    None of all the summer's train.

"All the buttercups—I bound them,
    And I robbed them of their gold.
All the cardinals—I found them,
    And I left them pale and cold.
Then I blew upon the roses,
    And their petals fell apart ;
Now each naked branch discloses
    Nothing but a bleeding heart.

"Golden-rods and daffodillies—
    How I laughed to see them go !
And I shook the dying lilies
    To the waters down below.

All the daisies lost their beauty,
    And the faded aster grieves.
Now I have no further duty
    But to toss the fallen leaves.

"I will raise such whirling masses -
    Why, hello! Now who are you,
Peeping from among the grasses,
    Like a little eye of blue?
You were hidden in your cover,
    And I must have passed you by.
Don't you know the summer's over,
    And it's time for you to die?"

"I was hiding from the breeze, sir,
    This is such a lonely spot;
I'm a little violet, please, sir,
    That the summer has forgot.
These tall grasses stood behind me,
    And the others all were gone,
So I think she couldn't find me,
    And she left me here alone.

" Me, of all the violets, only;
    And the birds all went along.
I am growing very lonely
    Here, without the robin's song.

For the days are dark and dreary,
  And the nights are long and cold ;
And I'm very, very weary,
  Since the sky has lost its gold.

" All the woods are wrapped in shadows,
  Every chirping thing is gone :
There's no sweetness in the meadows,
  And no music at the dawn.
I have missed the summer showers,
  And the rainbows in the sky ;
I'm the last of all the flowers,
  And I'm ready, sir, to die."

Then the Wind, who slew so blindly,
  That he'd spared no flowers yet,
Stooped and kissed her very kindly,
  Sighing, " Rest, poor Violet."
And he covered her completely
  With the leaves of red and gold,
And she lies there, sleeping sweetly,
  For she never feels the cold.

1885.

SLEIGHING SONG.

WE are gliding where the meadows
    In their crystal beauty glow;
Through the forest, where the shadows
    Lie asleep upon the snow;
Where the naked oaks, ashiver,
    Of the stinging cold complain
To the half-imprisoned river,
    Tearing at its icy chain.

Where the frozen brooklet lingers
    Till the winter's reign is o'er,
And the willows wring their fingers,
    As they crouch along the shore;
Through the silvery light that glances
    Where the mail-clad hills arise,
Till they shake their ashen lances
    In defiance at the skies.

Oh, was ever joy completer
    Than the sleighing time compels?
Was there ever music sweeter
    Than this singing of the bells?

Was there ever lighter motion
   Than this gliding of the sleigh,
Like a shallop on the ocean,
   With its wake of silver spray?

Not a cloud is in yon far height,
   As it arches, blue and fair,
And the frost, like frozen starlight,
   Trembles downward through the air ;
While the moon, above us hanging,
   Earthward turns her silver bow—
Don't you hear the arrows twanging,
   As they fall upon the snow?

Love may pine in melancholy,
   Where the tropic breezes blow ;
But he laughs to scorn such folly,
   As he flies above the snow,
Where the blood with very madness
   Through the bounding pulses wells,
And the heart in rhythmic gladness
   Times the music of the bells.

1878.

A DREAM OF SUMMER.

I LOVE, amid the winter's gloom,
  The joys of summer to recall:
Then fancy wafts me the perfume
  Of climbing roses on the wall,
Commingling with the fragrant breeze
  That, over blooming orchards borne,
Sighs softly through the maple trees,
  Or breathes among the waving corn.

Then, from the window of my room,
  I watch the snow-flakes in the air,
And fancy 'tis the locust bloom
  That falls, a fragrant shower there.
I close my eyes and fondly dream
  That winter's sighing sounds are all
But babblings of the summer stream,   '
  Or murmurs of the water-fall.

I dream of bearded, golden shocks
  That thickly stud the harvest plain,
Or merry bird, whose carol mocks
  The plowman whistling down the lane.

I see the sweet wild roses bend,
  Coquetting, to the stream's caress,
And hear the silvery tones that blend
  In praises of their loveliness.

I wake to find the summer past ;
  The locust bears a bloom of frost ;
The maple branches in the blast
  Like hanging skeletons are tossed.
The prisoned stream can sing no more,
  The water-fall has ceased to flow,
And where the roses lined the shore
  Are only briers crowned with snow.

1878.

HOME AND AFFECTION.

(43)

What to me the glittering treasure,
  Gathered from the mount of care!
Empty still must be the measure
  If no gems of love are there.
With the wealth of Home to bless me,
  I have riches all untold.
Let affection's arms caress me,
  And the mount may keep its gold.

Though ambition's flame may perish
  'Neath the ashes of the years,
While I hold the friends I cherish
  I am still too glad for tears.
If the mountain brambles wound them,
  Let who will ascend the trail,
I will tarry where I found them,
  Singing in the lowly vale.

FORTY YEARS OLD.

I AM forty to-day, but the heart of a boy
  In my bosom is pulsing away ;
My soul is so glad in its fullness of joy
  That I sing like a child at its play.
Life's morning of beauty I can not forget ;
  So fair was the day it foretold
That hues of its dawning encircle me yet,
  Though I know I am forty years old.

I know that the wrinkles should be on my brow,
  And that I should be sober and staid ;
But there is a laugh to smoothe over, somehow,
  Every furrow that sorrow hath made.
I can not be solemn and glum if I would,
  And the reason is easily told :
Each ill that arises I match with a good,
  And my pleasures are forty years old.

Perhaps I should delve into books like a ghoul,
  For the skeleton relics of thought,
But dearer to me is its fetterless soul
  That the book-makers never have caught.

I ramble the fields when the hues of the morn,
  Like the buds of the roses, unfold,
I mock the brown quail as it pipes in the corn,
  And forget I am forty years old.

Sometimes as I wander—to study inclined—
  A squirrel darts over my way ;
I toss back my locks, with a laugh, to the wind,
  And forget they are threaded with gray.
I shout like a boy, and away from my heart
  The weight of its sadness is rolled ;
I join in the chase, till I wake with a start,
  And remember I'm forty years old.

I sit at my door when the shadows go by,
  In their stealthy pursuit of the day ;
There comes to my side one whose merry blue eye
  Still can charm my heart shadows away.
We read the sweet story of love and of joy,
  That the years in their pages have told,
Till, wrapped in the twilight, the maid and the boy
  Never think they are forty years old.

I come to my home when the lamps are aglow—
  There's a charm in the hour for me—
I look for the one whose sweet presence I know,
  And lo ! I am welcomed by three.

The daughters, the mother, so like in their mien,
  That I pause in amaze to behold,
Till, filled with the joy and the peace of the scene,
  I am glad I am forty years old.

Though Time, the grim sexton, lays under the loam
  Full many a flower of bliss,
He never has breathed on a bloom of my home
  That Love has not saved with a kiss.
And now, when my record of sorrow and joy,
  Like a manuscript, backward is rolled,
I read through it all but the life of a boy
  With a happiness forty years old.
  1878.

JAQUELINE.

A H, they say we're growing old,
  But I know not what they mean.
Has your heart yet felt the cold,
          Jaqueline?

Nay, I read it in your eye;
  I am answered well, my queen.
Love hath given Age the lie,
          Jaqueline.

Time may spread the hair with gray,
  And the stately form may lean—
Hearts that love are young alway,
          Jaqueline.

He may spread the cheek with snow,
  And its roses he may glean—
Love can never perish so,
          Jaqueline.

Lean your head upon my breast;
  Lift to mine your eyes serene;
Love shall fancy all the rest,
          Jaqueline.

I shall see you as you stood—
  Ah, the years that intervene—
In your matchless womanhood,
            Jaqueline.

Stood that morn when life was young—
  All its trials unforeseen—
Where the climbing roses clung,
            Jaqueline.

In your eyes a tender light,
  Liquid as the dews of e'en ;
And your hair was like the night,
            Jaqueline.

One bold rose had dared to peep
  From its hiding place of green,
And you plucked it—Ah ! you weep,
            Jaqueline.

And you gave the rose to me,—
  Gave it with a stately mien ;
But your eyes I could not see,
            Jaqueline.

For they each, in swift eclipse,
  Hid behind a silken screen,
As I pressed it to my lips,
            Jaqueline.

And you stood in proud repose—
　　Stood as though you had not seen ;
But your cheek was like the rose,
　　　　　Jaqueline.

Then my soul was swift to leap,
　　Through a kiss, to Love's demesne.
Was it anger made you weep,
　　　　　Jaqueline?

Ah, though many, many a bliss
　　We have shared since then, my queen,
Heaven itself was in that kiss,
　　　　　Jaqueline.

And the fragrance of the rose
　　Sweetens all that lies between ;
And shall linger to the close,
　　　　　Jaqueline.

They can call us old who may.
　　Let them !　We have fared, I ween.
Hearts that love are young alway,
　　　　　Jaqueline.

1880.

BESSY AND JENNY.

B EST beloved of all my treasures,
    There are two I've set apart,
Shrined above my dearest pleasures
    On the altar of my heart.
And my thankful spirit blesses
    Him who formed them both so fair—
Bessy with the golden tresses,
    Jenny with the raven hair.

Bessy like the sunlight gleaming,
    As the hues of morning bright ;
Jenny like the starlight beaming,
    Calm and gentle as the night.
One where love must yield caresses,
    One where faith might kneel in prayer—
Bessy with the golden tresses,
    Jenny with the raven hair.

One with eyes of blue, and fairer
    Than the depth of summer skies ;
One with dark eyes, each a sharer
    In the light of Paradise.

Both with thousand tendernesses,
  Quick to smooth the brow of care—
Bessy with the golden tresses,
  Jenny with the raven hair.

All in vain affection measures
  Which is dearer, that or this ;
Both shall be my equal treasures,
  Love and faith be twins in bliss.
To the heart their presence blesses,
  Lord, in tender mercy spare
Bessy with the golden tresses,
  Jenny with the raven hair.

1879.

IF I WERE SISYPHUS.

IF I were Sisyphus, I know
    I would not labor long in vain,
Nor fret and wound my spirit so,
    To climb so far above the plain.
To reach the mountain height, I doubt
    That I have either heart or skill;
So I would turn myself about,
    And roll my burden down the hill.

There's beauty on the mountain top;
    The world of clouds is bright and fair;
But they who in the valley stop,
    Find peace and sweet contentment there.
'Tis brave to stand where grandeur towers
    Majestic on the peaks of snow;
But fame must climb above the flowers,
    And leave their sweetness all below.

He who would seek the upper air
    Must, like the eagle, soar alone,
And find the chill and silence there
    Turn blood to ice and heart to stone.

But he who loves the voice of song,
 And fain would hear the nightingale,
Must stop below, and tarry long,
 To find the singer in the vale.

Let others yearn and struggle long
 For plaudits of the coming years,
I would not give one thrush's song
 For all the music of the spheres.
I would not give one daisy flower
 For all the laurel-wreaths of Fame,
Nor change my quiet woodland bower
 For proud Ambition's altar-flame.

Though poverty may have its pains,
 Why should I scorn my humble cot,
Or why repine while love remains
 In gentle dalliance round the spot?
Why should I yearn for more, or shrink
 From Pride's disdain, or dread her sneers,
Since wealth, itself, must often drink
 The bitter water of its tears?

Then he who will may climb above
 For wealth or fame—I do not care.
I'll stay below with peace and love,
 And find my dearest treasure there.

I would not fret my spirit thus
    To reach a spot so bleak and chill ;
And so, if I were Sisyphus,
    I'd roll my burden down the hill.

1885.

TO MY WIFE.

WHY need you care, dear wife, or heed
    The passing of your early grace?
What though the lilies supersede
    The spring-time roses of your face?
What though the azure of your eyes
    Has mellowed to a softer blue?
The fairest tints that deck the skies
    Are caught from twilight's fading hue.

Why should the ripened fruit regret
    Its summer bloom, howe'er so fair?
Why should you sigh that Time has set
    His crown of silver on your hair?
The sweetest fragrance of the rose
    Is from its fading petals pressed,
And Nature spreads her earliest snows
    Above the flowers she loves the best.

What care we for the vanished years,
    Save for the fruit their summers brought?
What care we for our fallen tears,
    Save for the rainbows on them wrought?

Why should we mourn the joys we shared,
 Or see them perish with regret,
Since on the fruit our hearts have fared,
 And memory keeps the rainbows yet?

What though the winter time has come,
 And summer's buds and blooms expire?
Love hath an ever-radiant home,
 And bids us welcome to its fire.
He dwelt with us through all the spring ;
 We sheltered him from summer's heat ;
Now at his hearth we'll sit and sing,
 And let the wintry tempest beat.

1885.

AN EVENING PICTURE.

WHERE on the porch the sunlight gleams,
    Soft-sifted through the morning-glories,
The old man sits, like one who dreams,
    And tells his oft-repeated stories,
Till, growing mellow as the rays
    That turn his silver locks to golden,
He drones quaint songs of other days,
    And lives in memories, fond and olden.

Close to his side sweet blue-eyed May
    With circling arm he fondly presses,
His trembling fingers lightly play
    With laughing Katie's golden tresses.
Upon his knee sits romping Bess,
    And wonders why his tears have started ;
She can not know that last caress
    Was meant for one long since departed.

And now the sun's declining rays
    To glowing sheets of flame are turning ;
The western windows are ablaze,
    As if the houses all were burning ;

While May and Bessie laugh to see
  The red light gleam on Katie's tresses,
The old man, smiling at their glee,
  Bows down to meet their fond caresses.

Thus, if to me shall come the day
  When life has naught but oft-told stories,
And broken memories round me play
  Like sunlight through the morning-glories,
With loving hearts upon my breast,
  And loving arms about me twining,
May I, like him, as sweetly rest;
  As calmly see life's sun declining.

1878.

Retrospective.

(63)

When Memory lifts the misty veil
Which, like a shadow, seems to trail
   Above the hopes of vanished years,
Too oft we turn with mournful sigh
To count the graves wherein they lie,
   And see them through regretful tears.

Yet there are times when it is sweet
To stay our upward-climbing feet ;
   To lay care's weary burden down ;
And pausing thus, to fondly dream
That all things fair are what they seem,
   And Hope still wears her rosy crown.

Then to our inward sight arise
The vales of childhood's paradise ;
   The angel of the flaming sword,
That guards the gate from manhood's sin,
Turns half aside and lets us in
   To plead for pity from the Lord.

But by the path we must retrace
Stands many a stone to mark the place
  Where some dead aspiration sleeps.
And only those whose souls forget
Can chide the heart for its regret,
  Or mock at Memory when she weeps.

Hope, like the sun, must come and go ;
Her Orient must lose its glow,
  Its radiance be with darkness blent ;
And he who would have light alway
Must journey onward with the day
  To find it in the Occident.

But when our thriftless hands have spent
The legacy of life's intent,
  And Hope demands her parting dole,
'Tis sweet, amid the gathering gloom,
To find again the morning's bloom
  In evening's golden aureole.

(66)

THE HARVEST DAYS OF THE OLDEN TIME.

OH! the harvest days of the olden time!
    The ring of the sickles in merry rhyme!
The wealth that fell at the reaper's feet,
With the tinkling sound of a music sweet!
My soul is wrapped in a dream to-day,
And over my senses from far away
There comes a rustle of grain, combined
With the drowsy voice of the summer wind,
And my heart o'erflows with a song of praise
                    For the days—the days!
The harvest time of my boyhood days.

I stand again where the breezes toy
With the tangled locks of the farmer boy;
I hear the chorus of singing birds,
The tinkling bells of the grazing herds,
The happy shout and the joyous song,
And the gladsome laugh of the reaping throng;
The shout, the song and the merry peal,
Attuned to the ring of the flashing steel—
They come to me now through the dreamy maze
                    From the days—the days!
The harvest time of my boyhood days.

Again I walk in the joyous train
That follows after the loaded wain ;
Again to my heart, like an echo, come
The gladsome shouts of the harvest home,
When the merry, sun-browned lasses meet
The reaper lads with the golden wheat.
There was one, with hair of a sunnier hue
Than the ripened grain of the harvest knew,
Grew rosy as dawn at my ardent gaze
                In the days—the days !
The harvest time of my boyhood days.

Alas ! Alas ! how the years go by !
How the young grow old and the lovely die !
How sad the music, how marred the rhyme,
Of the harvest songs of the olden time !
For the rattling cog and the grinding wheel
Rise over the ring of the reaper's steel ;
And Death, the harvester, low hath laid
The golden hair of the sun-browned maid ;
And I sigh like one who vainly prays
                For the days—the days !
The vanished dream of my boyhood days.
1879.

AT THE MEADOW BARS.

WHAT little things can stir the heart,
  Though taught in care's benumbing school !
As dip of swallow wings will start
  The waves upon a sleeping pool,
Till widening round the sluggish meres
They break in laughter or in tears.

I found a withered flower to-day,
  Where youth had thrown such trifles by,
When first it learned that earth was clay,
  And heaven was far beyond the sky,
And with it, on my heart I found
The scar of this forgotten wound :—

'Twas in the time when Hope and Song
  Were wed, and in their honey-moon ;
When days of splendor sped along
  To nights of fairest plenilune ;
And mocking-birds along the hill
Loud oversang the whip-poor-will.

We stood beside the meadow bars,
  Where to our wondering sight arose
A host of dandelion stars
  Through milky-ways of elder blows,
So fair and bright that scarce we knew
The emerald heaven from the blue.

We talked of ways with pleasures sown ;
  How we should walk together there,
Till from the bloom of years was blown
  Its pollen dust upon our hair,
And life should, like the flowers, blend
To ripe fruition at the end.

And standing thus she gave the flower
  Which crumbles here to scentless dust.
" 'Tis mine," I cried, "to mark the hour
  When faith gave love sublimest trust."
And so we parted where we met,
To be forgotten—to forget.

I know not where she dwells to-day,
  In tropic clime, or land of snow :
Wedded or single, sad or gay,
  It moves me not, I only know
Not all the flowers from Love's demesne
Could bridge the gulf that lies between.

Ah, well! each heart must have its June—
Its love-dream at the meadow bars—
But they who reach the August noon
Shall miss the dandelion stars;
And whip-poor-wills alone be heard
Where earlier sang the mocking-bird.

1891.

I HAD.

I HAD a fair dream long ago ;
Heigho !
And the dawn was with beauty aglow,
I know.
But the glory is torn
From the brow of the morn,
And the dream and the glow—
They must go ;
Heigho !

I had a dear friend long ago ;
Heigho !
And affection hath shelter from woe,
I know.
But I found in my need
It was only a reed,
And the weight of my woe
Bent it low ;
Heigho !

I had a sweetheart long ago ;
Heigho !
And her soul was as pure as the snow,
I know.

My passion I told.
But another had gold,
And he melted the snow
   With its glow;
    Heigho!

I had a fond hope long ago :
    Heigho!
And the light of its beacon hung low,
    I know.
  Now, high and afar,
  It seems only a star,
  As I look from below
    For its glow;
    Heigho!

I had a light heart long ago :
    Heigho!
And trouble fell lightly as snow,
    I know.
  But the snow has grown deep,
  And the way is so steep,
  And my feet are so slow,
    As they go;
    Heigho!

I had an "*I have*" long ago ;

    Heigho !

And no sweeter hath life to bestow,

    I know.

But the world is so sad,

Since "*I have*" is "*I had*,"

And my tears blind me so,

    As they flow ;

    Heigho !

1879.

THE FLOWER AND THE STAR.

I HAD a flower that bloomed apart,
    In all its matchless loveliness.
I thought to wear it on my heart,
    To charm my spirit and to bless.

The lovely vale was all my pride ;
    The circling hills where steep and high ;
What cared we for the world outside ?
    We were content, my flower and I.

I clasped the bliss within my reach :
    My heart grew pure, my soul grew strong,
As thus we yielded, each to each,
    A wealth of fragrance and of song.

There was a blazing star that came
    To hang above our lovely vale ;
I gazed into its eye of flame,
    And all the world beside grew pale.

It thrilled my soul, it charmed my sight,
    And fragrance was no longer sweet.
I sprang to climb the rugged height,
    And crushed my flower beneath my feet.

The beetling crags subdued my will :
  The rocks were sharp and pitiless ;
The star went down behind the hill,
  And left me in my loneliness.

Bewildered, lost, I wandered far,
  And still must wander, sick with woe ;
I can not reach the vanished star,
  Nor find again my flower below.

1870.

KATE AND I.

WHEN we were children, Kate and I,
  She had the prettiest golden curls,
  And brightest eyes of all the girls ;
I stopped to gaze as she went by ;
  I tried to give her nuts and toys—
  She said she was afraid of boys—
When we were children, Kate and I.

When we were school-mates, Kate and I,
  I let her ride upon my sled,
  I brought her apples, large and red,
And wrote her lessons on the sly.
  I stood beside her in the class,
  And missed the words to let her pass,
When we were school-mates, Kate and I.

When we grew older, Kate and I,
  I walked beside her to the school,
  And blushed, and trembled like a fool,
And dared not meet her saucy eye.
  I tried to wrap her from the cold—
  She said I should not be so bold—
When we grew older, Kate and I.

When we were lovers, Kate and I,
   Her trusting faith was sweet to see,
   And she was all the world to me,
When we had sworn by earth and sky.
   Our vows were fond, we thought them true,
   And earth put on a brighter hue,
When we were lovers, Kate and I.

When we were parted, Kate and I,
   The weary miles were fraught with pain,
   And dragged between us like a chain—
Each link was welded with a sigh—
   Our letters passed, perhaps a score,
   Then slower came, then came no more,
And we were parted, Kate and I.

When we were married, Kate and I,
   It was not I that called her bride,
   It was not she who at my side
Looked wondering up to hear me sigh. '
   Come! Come! lie still, my foolish heart!
   Who thought we'd be so far apart
When we were married, Kate and I?

1878.

MY NATIVE VALLEY.

'TIS a thought that steals apart,
   Sweetly dreaming while it lingers—
 Dreaming of the long ago.
 'Tis a leaping of the heart
At the touch of Memory's fingers,
   Thrilling to a warmer glow.

 'Tis the music of a song,
Though too distant for completeness,
   Binding all my wayward will,
 While it bears my soul along,
Listening, yearning toward its sweetness,
   Drifting backward, backward still.

 Backward till the shadows lift,
And some mystic necromancy,
   Far beyond my spirit's ken,
 Sets the bark of Hope adrift,
While it wafts the sails of Fancy
   'Twixt the shores of Now and Then.

   *   *   *   *   *   *   *   *

Storied Susquehanna glides
Through one spot, from storms defended,
   Fair as day, yet calm as night.
There between the mountain sides,
Drowsy sound and sweetness blended,
   Flood the valley with delight.

Long ago the river's heart
Burst, and rent the hills asunder,
   That its prison walls had been ;
Then the mountains fell apart,
Shrinking back in startled wonder,
   And the lovely vale crept in.

Like a child o'erworn with play,
Now it dreamily reposes,
   Grown in beauty with the years ;
Fair to see and sweet alway,
Looking upward through the roses,
   Half in laughter, half in tears.

Over all a halo rests,
Lingering from the dawn's caressing,
   Ere her rosy lips grow pale,
When the chestnuts bowed their crests
To the morning's whispered blessing
   Breathing softly down the vale.

Upland oaks in stately pride
Frown upon the lowland beeches,
 Struggling to their prouder height;
 Cedars, on the mountain side,
Upward climb in purple reaches,
 Melting in the amber light.

Sunlit seas of waving wheat,
Rosy bays of clover meadows,
 Sweep along the far hill's side;
 White-bloomed orchards at their feet
Rest within the purple shadows,
 Nestling sweetly as a bride.

Music weaves her thousand spells,
Where the glad heart of the fountain
 Drips its laughter down the walls,
 And the soul of beauty dwells
In the grottoes of the mountains,
 Silver-veiled with water-falls.

Thus the picture rises fair—
Rises to my inward vision,
 Rapturous as a poet's theme;
 And my spirit wanders there
Glad as souls through fields elysian
 Sometimes wander in a dream.

Then my weary, yearning heart
Leaps at touch of Memory's fingers,
Thrilling to a warmer glow ;
And a thought will steal apart,
Sweetly dreaming as it lingers
Down the vales of long ago.

1879.

REMINISCOR, DEPLORO.

I REMEMBER well when Time
  Dragged his feet in leaden shoon ;
And the sluggard day did climb
  All too slowly to the noon—
    Heigho! the burning noon!
Now his stride is swift and long ;
  Westward speeds the flying day ;
Morning's ecstacies of song,
  Morning's visions—where are they?
    Well-a-day, ah, well-a-day!

I remember when the sky
  Seemed to touch the distant wood ;
And the gold that used to lie,
  Where the rainbow arches stood—
    Heigho! how fair they stood!
Now my eyes grow dim with pain,
  Heaven seems so far away—
Hope and faith alike in vain—
  And the treasures—where are they?
    Well-a-day, ah, well-a-day!

I remember, with a sigh,
  One who was my earliest friend ;
How we vowed to live and die
  True heart-brothers to the end—
    Heigho ! the bitter end !
But the eager grasp for gain
  Tore the golden cord away.
Heart and soul have felt the pain,
  But the riches—where are they?
    Well-a-day, ah, well-a-day !

I remember once, when Fame
  Sought my spirit to beguile.
On her scroll she wrote a name,
  And I blessed her for a smile—
    Heigho ! the cruel smile !
Low I bent before her shrine,
  But she turned her face away,
And the name—it was not mine—
  Hope and promise—where are they ?
    Well-a-day, ah, well-a-day !

I remember, ah, too well,
  All this heart-ache and regret.
Would that I could break the spell ;
  Would that memory could forget—
    Heigho ! *could* she forget?

I have journeyed since the morn,
    Over many a flowery way ;
This I know—my hands are torn,
    But the roses—where are they ?
        Well-a-day, ah, well-a-day !

1879.

MY CASTLE.

I BUILT me a castle, strong-portaled and high ;
   Its minarets pierced to the dome of the sky ;
Its towers were crowned with the clouds overhead ;
Its battlements bannered with purple and red.
       It stood by a stream
          That was crystal as truth ;
       It was built in a dream,
          In the time of my youth ;
And I said to myself, I will shut myself in,
And laugh at the arrows of sorrow and sin.

Its ditches were wide, and I set them afloat ;
Its portals were guarded by drawbridge and moat ;
My sword was unsheathed, and my banners unfurled,
And my bugle blew challenge out into the world.
       I laughed as I thought
          How the story would run,
       When the battle was fought
          And the victory won—
That safe in assault from all pillage and ruth,
My valor had kept the fair castle of youth.

Alas ! my defiance and valor were vain.
A host of grim warriors came over the plain.
They waded the moat, they ascended the wall ;
They captured the battlements, banners and all.

   My weapons were cast
    To the earth as I fled,
   And the arrows fell fast
    On the way that I sped.

Oh, heart-hurts are sore, but my sorrow and dole
Are deeper for wounds in the wings of my soul.

That castle—last night I beheld it again ;
A ruin it stands in the midst of the plain.
Foul things are creeping about in the hall,
And owlets are hatched on the battlement wall.

   The vale is beset,
    And with bugle and hounds
   The foe tracks me yet
    By the blood of my wounds.

Alas ! for the castle I built by the stream !
I visit it only by stealth—when I dream.
 1886.

THE CLOUD-SHIP.

BEHOLD how she sails—the fair ship of the sky—
　　Where the breakers a-port and a-lee
Are dashed into foam on the islands that lie
　　On the verge of yon aureate sea !
A crimson-hulled shallop, with canvas of snow,
　　Distent to the breeze that impels her along ;
And Hope is the pilot—her pennant I know,
For she brought me a ship in the long, long ago
　　From the far-away regions of song.

I saw her afar like a sun-lighted cloud,
　　And I joyfully hailed from the shore,
But out on the waters the breakers were loud,
　　And the answer was lost in their roar.
The freight was more precious than jewels or gold,
　　That came from those beautiful regions for me ;
I saw her go down, and I wept to behold,
For only the wreck of the cargo was rolled
　　To the shore by the pitiless sea.

Like the ship of my hopes, yonder vessel is frail,
  And the tempest that follows behind,
Outspeeds her, o'ertakes her, and cordage and sail
  Float away on the wings of the wind.
Now, drifting dismantled, her voyage is o'er ;
  Woe ! woe ! to the hearts that her coming await !
For long will they watch, as I watch, evermore,
But Hope can not pilot her bark to the shore,
  And the sea shall deliver her freight.

  1877.

THE SPRING BY THE WILLOWS.

THERE'S a spring that I love in my far-away home,
  Where the sunshine of happiness ripened my heart;
And I hear its sweet music wherever I roam,
  And its song of my song shall be ever a part.
It flowed from the bank where the willow-trees grew,
  And the merry thrush sang to his image below;
Where the wild roses bloomed with a lovelier hue,
  Than elsewhere, in all the world, roses can know.

There the light of the sun had a mellower gleam,
  And the cowslips were richer in treasures of gold;
There the summer winds whispered of love to the
      stream,
  That sang low to itself the sweet story they told,
Till a murmur of restfulness dwelt in its tide,
  And the violets nodded there all the day long;
And the happy boy-dreamer lay down by its side,
  To be soothed into sleep by its lullaby song.

But, alas! for the distance! alas! for the years!
  It comes to me now like a whisper of prayer;
For the moan of my sorrow is loud in my ears,
  And the dust of the journey lies white on my hair.

But I lean, like a lover, who listens, alone,
  To the dear one who sings from her window at
    night,
Still happy to catch but a wandering tone,
  And blessed by the fragments of broken delight.
  1880.

WILLOW WHISTLES.

'TWAS long ago—'tis but a dream—
    Enwoven like a silver thread
In emerald velvet, wound the stream
    Through meadow-lands with daisies spread ;
Where flaming dandelions grew,
    And shone like gold among the green,
And violets with eyes of blue
    Peeped shyly out upon the scene :—

A barefoot boy and sun-browned lass
    Sat making whistles by the brook :
The willows at the nodding grass
    Their sun-lit tresses gayly shook ;
The rushes bowed in yielding ranks
    Where wooing winds of summer sighed,
And white-robed hawthorns on the banks
    Embraced above the silvery tide.

Not purer flowed from Helicon
    The fabled fount of Hippocrene,
Than this fair streamlet, singing on
    Between its banks of gold and green.

The harp of Orpheus never filled
  The listening nymphs with sweeter joy
Than from the willow whistle thrilled
  Along the pulse of maid and boy.

And thus flew by the light-winged hours,
  While on the stream in childish play
They cast their broken twigs and flowers,
  And as they watched them drift away.
They dreamed that Time, in coming years,
  Would gently bear their lives along,
Where love's sweet light on sorrow's tears
  Arch rainbows over vales of song.

But gliding like that singing stream
  The passing years sweep ever on :
And hopes that filled their loving dream
  Are, like the drifting flowers, gone.
He flung his boyhood's toy away
  To listen to the trump of fame ;
And she forgot the merry lay
  That from the willow whistle came.

The willow died ; the nodding grass
  And rushes are no longer there :
The fickle winds have sought. alas !
  And wooed a thousand scenes as fair.

And he, recalling like a dream
   That summer day, has often sighed
That one as lovely as the stream
   Should prove as changeful as its tide.

The hawthorn stands where then it stood—
   No flower or leaf its head adorns—
She wears her crown of womanhood,
   And finds it but a crown of thorns.
And he, 'mid sorrow's blasting flame,
   Has seen his clould-built castles fall,
And finds, alas! the trump of fame
   A willow whistle after all.

1878.

Sorrow and Bereavement.

There is no heart but has its woe,
  However strong the pulse may beat ;
There is no path by which we go,
  But thorns will lie beneath our feet ;
There is no day, howe'er so fair,
  But round its rim some clouds will sweep ;
No life without some sepulcher,
  Where Love must stop to weep.

But oft the veil of doubts and fears
  By Sorrow's trembling hand is riven :
And through the lenses of our tears
  We get a closer view of Heaven.
The stoic soul is stung to prayer
  By clods that on a coffin fall ;
And hearts are taught by their despair
  That God is over all.

DEAD.

YE little griefs that fret and fume
    About the portals of the heart,
  Away! away! there is no room!
    This sorrow claimeth every part.
  Ye cares that wait on Fortune's frown,
    To plague me with your spiteful wings,
    Ye now are insects void of stings,
     And light as thistle-down.

  Ye puny drops, so quick to tell
    Of little woes and little fears,
  When every pebble-pain that fell
    Could stir the shallow fount of tears,
  Ye were but summer rains, and warm,
    With sunlight hues among them blent.
    Alas! no rainbow arch is bent
     Above this winter storm.

  For she is dead—all else is naught—
    One boundless, measureless abyss—
  But yesterday my soul was caught
    Up to the very doors of bliss;

Ah, woe is me! no falling star,
    Cast downward from its high estate,
    E'er sped so swift from Heaven's gate,
    Or sank through night so far.

Oh, vanished Hope, whose pinions flashed
    One little moment in my sight!
With face upturned and tempest-dashed,
    I gaze into the boundless night,
And see no ray of Heaven there.
    In vain I strive to pierce the gloom—
    My sight is prisoned in a tomb,
    And fettered by despair.

Let grandeur dwell within the wood,
    And vales be filled with bloom and light;
Let splendor flush the rose's blood,
    And dew-drops wash the lilies white;
I heed them not, nor care to find
    Nor grace nor beauty anywhere.
    He recks not that the world be fair
    Whom grief hath stricken blind.

The sweetest tones of Music's shell
    Have lost their charm to soothe my soul.
I only hear a sobbing bell,
    That seems to toll, and toll, and toll.

In vain the fancy I forbid;
  I hear it still, and over all
  The hollow sound of clods that fall
    Upon a coffin lid.

Oh, soul, that plumed thy wings for flight,
  To learn the music of the spheres!
Oh, heart, so full of earth's delight
  Thou hadst no chamber for its tears!
Hope with her beacon star hath fled
  Into a tomb, where now ye wait,
  Like watchers at the charnal gate,
    The dead beside the dead.

1885.

NORA.

THOU art dead, and I am lonely,
　　Oh, so lonely in my sorrow!
Anguish now, and anguish only,
　　When the sun shall rise to-morrow—
　　　Rise to mock the tears I shed.
Tarry, sun, for I am hiding,
　　Grief and I our vigil keeping;
Stay, oh night, for thy abiding
　　Shameth not my bitter weeping—
　　　Weeping for my dead.

Hide, oh kindly shadows, hide me,
　　For the world is all unfeeling.
Memory, bow thyself beside me,
　　Thou and I together kneeling—
　　　Kneeling in the night alone.
"Nora, Nora, art thou near me?"
　　Yearningly my spirit calleth.
"Nora, Nora, canst thou hear me?"
　　On my heart the silence falleth—
　　　Falleth like a stone.

Like a mateless dove my spirit
   Seeketh thee in realms immortal.
Nora, Nora, canst thou hear it
   Beat its wings against the portal—
     Beat and plead for entrance there?
" Nora, Nora, I am lonely,
   Oh, so lonely, love, without thee !
Nora, Nora !" Silence only—
   Silence and despair about me
     Dwelleth every-where.

1880.

TOM MAY.

"DEAD!" the wailing night winds cry!
  "Dead!" the sobbing vales are calling,
    From the darkness, far away.
"Dead!" the whispering woods reply,
  Till my hot tears all seem falling
    Inward on my heart, Tom May.

Dead! alas! my more than friend!
  Gone from me beyond returning!
    Could not love your flight delay?
Must I linger to the end,
  Groping still with tear-blind yearning
    For your vanished hand, Tom May?

Ah! 'twas many years ago,
  When our friendship first we plighted,
    Where the dead between us lay;
For we both had loved him so—
  He, the hero Death had knighted
    On that field of blood, Tom May.

There we dug his shallow grave,—
  You and I—no martial dirges
    Wailed above the new-heaped clay;
But the night-wind mourned the brave,
  And the Rappahannock's surges
    Sang his requiem, Tom May.

Thus we stood, your hand in mine,
  Mid a silence all unbroken;
    For we found no word to say;
But, like goblets brimmed with wine,
  Heart touched heart in loving token,
    Pledged for all the years, Tom May.

Now I reach my hand again,
  But no loving touch replying,
    Lifts my heart above the clay.
I am standing now as then,
  But the grave between us lying
    Shuts you from my sight, Tom May.

Close below my feet you lie,
  Yet the tears that wet my lashes
    Make you seem so far away!
Oh, my friend, that you should die!
  God! must Death resolve to ashes
    Such a heart as yours, Tom May?

I shall see the world go by—
 See each little trickster creeping
  On his victim to betray.
Oh, that life should keep the lie,
 While the soul of truth is sleeping,
  Silent in your grave, Tom May.

Spiteful bats that love the night—
 Why, O Death, are these untaken?
  Oh, my eagle of the day,
Stricken midway in your flight!
 Honor's eyrie seems forsaken,
  Now that you are dead, Tom May.

Dead, alas! and love in vain
 Strives to quicken with its yearning
  Heart of dust and lips of clay!
Cold and silent they remain.
 Gone from me beyond returning!
  Oh! my heart is sore. Tom May.

1885.

THE EMPTY NEST.

A ROBIN came
With the day's last flame,
To the maple tree beside my door.
She sought her nest,
But below her breast
Were the fallen leaves, and nothing more.

All summer long,
What a gush of song
She poured to welcome the coming dawn!
Now the song is still,
And her heart is chill,
For her mate and her nestlings—all are gone.

Oh, robin mother!
I know another,
Whose nestlings flew when their wings grew strong.
Now she sits alone,
Where the chill winds moan,
With a heart, like thine, too sad for song.

Like thee, she turns
To the past, and yearns
For those who nestled against her breast;
But the days go by,
And her dead hopes lie,
Like fallen leaves in her empty nest.

1885.

THE TWO MOTHERS.

TWO mothers stand by the earth, new-piled,
　　Where the grave-yard grass was wont to wave;
One looks, fond-eyed, on her smiling child,
　　But one looks into an open grave.

And both are weeping—the one with grief,
　　That rends her soul with a sore distress;
And one for pity, in part, but chief
　　From the sense of her heart's deep thankfulness.

She hears the wail and the startled cry,
　　At the hollow sound when the clods fall in,
And she clasps her child with a choking sigh—
　　"Oh, God! Oh, God! If it should have been!"

Two mothers come in the after years
　　And stand by the side of that grave again;
But Time, who chastens the mourner's tears,
　　Has brought to the other a tearless pain.

The one looks up from the sculptured stone,
　　With yearning eyes, to the sky o'erhead;
But ah! the other makes bitter moan,
　　For her dear one lost—and yet not dead.

She wrings her hands in her dark despair,
  For one astray in the paths of sin;
And she cries as she kneels by the small grave there,
  "Oh, God! Oh, God! that it might have been!"
1885.

BUT YESTERDAY.

BUT yesterday I was a child;
   But yesterday the earth I trod
Seemed all as fair as when it smiled
   At the creative kiss of God.
   (I had not learned that earth was clay.)
   Then Joy his gladsome pean rang,
And Faith walked hand in hand with me ;
   Then Hope, the siren, sweetly sang,
On somewhere, in the yet to be,
   But yesterday! but yesterday!

But yesterday my darkest fears
   Were clouds that wore a silver crest ;
My deepest sorrows dried their tears,
   And slept upon my mother's breast.
   (I knew not then of love's decay.)
   My mother dear, no later bliss
Hath ever healed affliction's smart.
   Oh, could I feel again the kiss
That drew the sorrow from my heart,
   But yesterday! but yesterday!

But yesterday and life was sweet,
  And not a shadow o'er it fell.
I cast my heart at Friendship's feet,
  And thought that she would love it well.
(I had not learned that friends betray.)
  But Envy's bitter vintage drips
In Pleasure's wine, and Friendship's smile
  Burned into curses on the lips
That gave their kisses to beguile,
  But yesterday! but yesterday!

But yesterday the world was wide,
  From height to height expanding still.
I ran my course with gallant stride,
  And all its ways were at my will.
(I thought it would be thus alway.)
  But, bruised by many a cruel fall,
My soul is hopeless now to win ;
  My pathway stops against a wall
That blinds my sight and shuts me in,
  And hides the hopes of yesterday.

1870.

THE SONG OF THE RAIN.

WHEN first my heart bled with its sorrow,
    I sat all the night with my pain,
And heard, like a wail for the dying,
    The funeral song of the rain.

I wrapped myself up in the shadows ;
    For Faith from my spirit had fled,
And Hope stood afar in the darkness,
    To weep with the rain for my dead.

But now, as I hear at my window
    The touch of those fingers so light,
That weave in the warp of the silence
    The woof of their music to-night,

So sweet is the sound and so restful
    The charm which its melody brings,
That sorrow has folded her pinions,
    To listen while memory sings.

And all that my soul has been dreaming
The rain in its music repeats,
While thoughts, that, like bees, have been roam-
ing,
Come bearing their burden of sweets.

Now Faith paints the bow of her promise
On tear-drops that sorrow has shed,
And Love is beguiled from her mourning,
And turns from the grave of her dead.

And Hope, like a carrier pigeon,
Though weary and torn by the blast,
Escaping the snare of the fowler,
Flies home with her message at last.

For now, as I list to the fingers
That harp on my window to-night,
I hear from the rim of the darkness
The voices that sing of the light.

1877.

FLIGHTS OF FANCY.

(115)

When I was young, I tuned my song
  To suit the deeper tones of age ;
And oft I did my muse a wrong
  To ape the wisdom of the sage.
I longed to see each springing shoot
  A stately tree within the hour,
And, too impatient for the fruit,
  I missed the sweetness of the flower.

Now I am old, I love to cheat
  My sorrow with a gladder strain ;
And find a thousand fancies sweet,
  That youth o'erleaped in proud disdain.
And thus, when gentler memories throng
  About my heart, am I beguiled
To weave with manhood's later song
  The rippling laughter of the child.

THE WIND THAT KISSED THE ROSE

OR

THE SCANDAL IN THE GARDEN.

ALL the garden was astonished
At the scandal running there ;
All the mother-flowers admonished
All their daughters to beware ;
Every pretty pansy pouted
Underneath her Quaker hood,
And the peonies fairly shouted
With amazement where they stood.

And the poppies from their languor
Seemed to waken for a spell,
When the columbines in anger
Clattered every purple bell.
While nasturtiums, stern in duty,
· Leaned against the garden wall,
And each portulacca beauty
Shut her crimson parasol.

All the larkspurs in their places
Grew as blue as blue could be ;
And the sunflowers turned their faces,
That they might not seem to see.

(119)

And the modest morning-glory
  Hastened all her ears to close,
When she heard the dreadful story,
  That the Wind had kissed the Rose.

Oh! was ever such a scandal
  In the garden heard before?
And the Wind the saucy vandal
  They would countenance no more;
And the wanton rose should rue it
  Till the moment of her death.
There was no mistake they knew it,
  For they smelled it on his breath.

And in virtuous indignation,
  How they toss their pretty heads,
As the terrible relation
  Round about the garden spreads!
But their modest daisy sister,
  When she heard them all condemn,
Wondered how they knew he kissed her,
  If he wasn't kissing them.

1893.

LOVE'S HOLIDAY.

O F Duty's school impatient grown,
   'Tis said that Love, one sunny morn,
Ran on his truant way alone,
Through meadow lands with daisies strewn,
By banks with dandelions sown,
   And fields of tasseled corn.

How sweet his stolen holiday !
   All unrestrained by curb or rule,
His vagrant feet were free to stray.
He sang : "Oh, Love should roam alway,
And only Virtue, grim and gray,
   Should sit in Duty's school."

And so in happiness complete,
   He followed every shining prize.
He roused the hare from her retreat ;
He mocked the quail among the wheat ;
And ran with eager, heedless feet,
   To chase the butterflies.

But Folly, playing with her bell,
  Sat in the wood beside the way.
She lured him onward by its spell,
Till in a deep and thorny dell,
She left him crying where he fell,
  And mocked him as he lay ;

Till Wisdom came with stately pace
  And solemn mien along the glen.
With frowning brow, but touch of grace,
She led him from the tangled place ;
But Love was frightened at her face,
  And took to flight again.

Then Pleasure came across the plain,
  Bedecked with garments rich and bright ;
About her throat a golden chain,
And on her lips a ruddy stain,
Where purple lees of wine had lain
  Through all the wassail-night.

Love thought her pure as she was fair,
  Nor saw her smile was half in scorn—
Her voice of laughter half despair—
Till, as he sprang, her kiss to share,
The roses tangled in her hair
  Transfixed him with a thorn.

Then from her brow the wreath she tore,
  And broke the clasp that held her chain.
Alas! her charms enticed no more ;
Love gazed, his fond illusion o'er,
And saw behind the mask she wore,
  The furrowed face of pain.

Where Beauty, 'neath her garden bower
  In pensive sweetness sat apart,
Love paused ; his grief confessed a power
Like sunlight falling through a shower,
And bending low he begged a flower
  To wear upon his heart.

Then Beauty rose with gracious air,
  To give a blossom nothing loth ;
She plucked the one she deemed most fair ;
They bowed their heads its breath to share.
Alas! a bee was ambushed there,
  And stung the lips of both.

Poor Beauty wailed her hapless fate—
  But seemed the fairer as she cried—
When down the walk came frowning Hate,
And fiercely shut the garden gate,
While Love was left in woeful state
  Upon the outer side.

But as he stood in sore dismay
   At Beauty's wrath, so slow to cool,
Bewailing all the sad array
Of griefs that marred his holiday,
Grim Virtue came along that way
   And led him back to school.

And ever since that luckless day—
   So all the legends do declare—
Love takes no stolen holiday,
And never has been known to stray.
Not even "just across the way,"
   Unless in Virtue's care.

Which may be true—as legends go—
   It forms no portion of my task
To give you answer, yes or no,
Or prove that Love is pure as snow :
But he, himself, will tell you so,
   If you will only ask.

But since my story needs must bear
   A moral, lest your fancy roam
On Love's escape from Duty's care,
And not enough on his despair :
I give you this : Let Love beware
   Of going far from home.

1893.

THE BATTLE OF THE WIND AND THE CORN.

THE Winds were a wild and vandal host,
  The robbers of woodland bowers,
And laden with all things sweet, but most
  With the breath of ravished flowers.
The Corn was a brave and gallant band,
  Disdaining the robber's spoil,
But rich with wealth of the fruitful land,
  To gladden the heart of toil.

All night the Winds in ambush lay,
  In the depths of the upland wood ;
All night the Corn in its brave array,
  In the shades of the valley stood.
No bivouac fire on the hill was seen,
  No light in the valley camp,
And none by the stream that ran between,
  Save the flash of the fire-fly's lamp.

But when the birds in the woodland bowers
  Awakened on vine and tree,
The Winds blew into the trumpet-flowers,
  And sounded the reveille.

And their stragglers hurried to and fro,
  To plunder the clover blooms,
While the marshaled host in the vale below
  Stood tossing their knightly plumes.

For undismayed in their battle line
  Was the host of the valiant Corn,
And their hearts were strong with the dewy wine,
  From the rosy cup of morn.
Ten thousand swords, all flashing bright,
  Were drawn for the coming fray;
Ten thousand pennons were dancing light
  In the glow of the dawning day.

Then the Winds in dashing and wild array
  Came charging across the vale,
And the grass was beaten along the way
  As with blows of a mighty flail.
But the brave green guardians of the plain—
  They battled long and well,
And many a foeman shrieked with pain
  Where their cimeters rose and fell.

Then the Winds dashed fiercely through the field,
  And the roar of the battle-tide,
With shiver of blade and clash of shield,
  Swept on to the farther side.

Then out and on, with a laugh of scorn,
They fled to the forest gloom ;
But the sun that looked on the gallant Corn
Saw many a tattered plume.

1893.

CUPID AND DEATH.*

ONE day two rival hunters met—
   'Twas human hearts they both pursued—
The one was Death, with visage set
   In terror's fierce similitude ;

And one was Cupid, fair with grace
   Of rosy cheeks and laughing eyes.
They oft had crossed upon the chase,
   And struggled for the self-same prize.

But now this covenant they made :
   All rivalry would each forego,
And one should hunt the upland glade,
   And one, the gloomy vale below.

So Cupid lay in ambush where
   An arch of roses twined above,
And, waiting for the young and fair,
   He pierced their hearts with wounds of love.

*There are two versions of this fable. John G. Saxe has woven one
of them into rhyme. I have taken the liberty to use the other.

But Death went down into the vale
  And dwelt within a gloomy cave ;
And oft the cheek of age grew pale,
  While passing by a new-made grave.

But Cupid left the glade one day,—
  Grown tired of the rose's breath—
And, wandering to the vale, he lay
  Asleep within the cave of Death.

The quiver at his side fell o'er,
  And all his arrows tumbled out,
And lay where Death upon the floor
  Had strewn his poisoned darts about.

At length he woke, but who can tell
  The evil in that moment done?
He grasped his arrows where they fell,
  And some were Death's and some his own.

And now he speeds his mingled darts,
  And finds them oft unfaithful prove,
And carry death to youthful hearts
  That should have felt the shaft of love.

And Death, himself, oft sees, with rage,
  His arrows fail to stop the breath,
And wound with love the heart of age
  That should have felt the shaft of death.

1879.

JOY AND SORROW.

ONE morning Joy and Sorrow
    Set forth at earliest peep of day,
To journey till the morrow
    Along a fair and flowery way.
But Sorrow was infirm and old ;
    Much weeping, too, had made him blind ;
And Joy was supple, young and bold,
    And soon he left his mate behind.
He plucked of fruit and flower
    And found them all exceeding sweet,
Till in a rosy bower
    He fell asleep at Pleasure's feet.

Alas ! while Joy was sleeping,
    Unmindful of the waning day,
Came Sorrow, slowly creeping,
    And passed before him on the way.
Then brambles o'er the pathway spread,
    Where only roses grew before,
And Joy, awaking, vainly sped ;
    He never passed by Sorrow more.

And now he seeks no bower,
　But trace of Sorrow's step appears,
And finds no fruit or flower
　But bears the blight of Sorrow's tears.

1885.

THE BIRTH OF POESY.

WHILE yet the world, but newly born,
    Lay silent in the lap of night,
Far up the east the gates of morn
    Were opened to the coming light.
Then Music, "maid of heavenly birth,"
    Beheld the dusky gates withdrawn,
And took her truant flight to earth,
    Along the pathway of the dawn.

She wandered through the dewy grove,
    And hung a harp on every tree ;
She taught the birds their songs of love,
    And gave the waters melody.
O'er hill and vale she lightly sped,
    Surrounded by a tuneful throng,
Till Silence woke, and, frightened fled,
    And all the earth was filled with song.

It chanced that Fancy idly strayed
    Along the vale that fragrant morn,
He met, he wooed, he won the maid,
    They wed, and Poesy was born.

A restless sprite, with Music's soul
  Attuned to sweetest harmonies,
But Fancy's will that spurns control,
  And all his glowing phantasies.

Now, with what thrilling raptures fraught
  The witching strains he pours along,
When weaving Fancy's glittering thought
  Amid the golden threads of song!
When shall a richer gift be given
  Than that which mingled in his birth?—
The best, the sweetest part of heaven,
  With all that's beautiful of earth.

1886

THE INTERPRETER.

A THOUGHT sped through the land,
　　On swift and airy wing,
And none could grasp or understand
　　The bright inconstant thing.
Some said, " It is of pleasure born,"
　　And some, " 'Tis child of pain."
" 'Tis joyous as a summer morn ;"
　　" 'Tis sad as midnight rain."
" Who will interpret it ? " they cried,
　　" This airy thing that mocks us so ? "
" Alas ! ", they each to each replied,
　　" We feel, but do not know."

Then Music took her shell
　　And blew so sweet a strain,
The Thought was prisoned by the spell,
　　And bound as with a chain.
" Behold ! " they cried, " the charm is found ;
　　Bring gems and gold to her
Who holdeth in melodious sound
　　The Thought's interpreter."

And all the people ran with speed
    Their richest offerings to bestow—
" Alas ! " they cried, " the sounds recede ;
    We hear, but do not know."

Then God-like Sculpture smote
    The rock before his face,
And on its polished surface wrote
    In lines of living grace.
" The mystery is here," they said,
    " The Thought is carved in stone ; "
And came with bared and bended head,
    Like vassals to a throne.
" Well hath the sculptor won the prize."
    They cried,—" But still it mocks us so !
There hangs a veil before our eyes—
    We see, but do not know."

Then Painting next essayed
    To catch the flitting thing,
And on his magic canvas spread
    All hues that tint the spring.
And men were eager to behold,
    And Rumor mouthed his name,
And willing thousands brought their gold
    To fill his crown of fame.

But as they gazed they, sighing, said,
　" Alas ! must it be ever so?
The Thought is uninterpreted,
　For still we do not know."

An humble Poet wrought
　Beside his sick child's bed,
And all men read, and lo ! the Thought
　At last interpreted !
Its sweetness gladdened all the land,
　And cheered the heart like wine.
The Poet kissed the poor, dead hand,
　That stung his lips with brine :
And on his lonely way he sighed,
　For men went by him with a smile.
" What hath the Poet earned?" they cried,
　" *We knew it all the while.*"

1890.

THE SOUL'S VOYAGE.

A SOUL came halting to the strand
   That bounds Death's dark and silent sea,
With Hope and Love on either hand,
   And Faith before to guide the three.

Long had they journeyed through the world,
   Where woe and pain in ambush lay,
And many a shaft of sin was hurled
   To wound the Soul upon its way.

And oft had it been sorely grieved ;
   Oft Hope her cheering song forgot ;
E'en Faith, at times, but·half believed,
   And only Love had faltered not.

But now their pilgrimage was o'er,
   Hope bade the fainting Soul be brave,
While Faith stood pointing from the shore,
   To one low star across the wave.

But Love, with gentle hand, led on
   To where was moored a shining bark ;
And all the sea grew red with dawn,
   Though all the shores of earth were dark.

Then, as the sky grew bright above,
    They steered to meet the morning star—
They two, alone, for only Love
    Could sail across the harbor bar.

1893.

ECHOES OF WAR TIME.

When first along our Southern shore
 There rolled the sound of battle crashing,
A thousand flags leaped, fluttering, o'er
 A hundred thousand bayonets flashing.
   The farmer quit the half-turned soil;
   The village artisan his toil;
The merchant left his wares unsold
 To fill his place among the trenches;
The lawyer kept his plea untold,
 That else had fallen on empty benches.

And hands that knew no rougher touch
 Than whip or rein, took up the saber;
The very cripple cursed his crutch,
 In envy of his stalwart neighbor.
   The banker left his golden store,
   And men of books forgot their lore,
And threw the garb of peace aside,
 The bliss of home and love foregoing,
While southward rolled the battle's tide,
 'Twixt gulf and ocean, ebbing, flowing.

Ebbing and flowing through the years
 That love from love in anguish parted;
That dimmed the brightest eyes with tears,
 And left the merriest broken-hearted;
   That filled our Northern vales with dead;
   That dyed our Southern rivers red;

(141)

That hung a cloud of gloom and woe,
   In sullen blackness o'er the Nation,
And shut from tearful eyes the glow
   Of Freedom's scattered constellation.

So true in love! so brave in war!
   Why should the world forget their story?
Some vanished like a falling star,
   That leaves behind a trail of glory.
      Some followed Fame, with eager chase,
      And clasped her in their dead embrace,
But many a heart that found her not
   In some forgotten grave reposes,
And but the night-wind knows the spot,
   And scatters there its tribute roses.

For many years the palm of peace
   Has stretched its grateful arms to Heaven,
(Long may it flourish and increase,
   By war's dread lightning never riven,
      But who shall chide if hands should clasp
      Each other yet with eager grasp,
When men recall the war-drum's roll,
   The clash of steel, the musket's rattle,
Where heart to heart and soul to soul
   Were welded by the fire of battle?

ROLL CALL.

[Read at a camp-fire of the G. A. R.]

THE bugle sounds ! Fall in ! Fall in !
   Close up ! Right dress ! So, steady ! Front !
Sergeant, the lines are formed ; begin
   To call the roll as you were wont
In those rough days of long ago,
   Ere these young men and maids were born,
As from the past floats soft and low
   The music of the bugle horn.

And with its echoes seems to rise
   A vision of the vanished years,
Till o'er that twilight landscape lies
   The dew of memory's silent tears.
The vanished years when stalwart men
   Touched elbows down the long blue line,
And charged through Southern wood and glen,
   Till earth was drunk with Death's red wine.

Ay, redder wine than e'er was crushed
   From purple grapes, and richer far,
Was trod from hero hearts, and gushed
   About the crimson feet of War.

(143)

And pangs that time can ne'er assuage
   Were gathered then for all the years,
On fields new named for history's page,
    Whose christening font o'erflowed with tears.

That long blue line ! how swift it sprang
   In answer to the bugle peal !
That charging shout ! how loud it rang
   Along the ranks of leveled steel !
What gallant souls flew up to God !
   What hero hearts amid the fray,
Poured rich libation on the sod
   Where now they mingle, clay with clay !

Ay, there was manhood, tall and swart,
   With strength of limb and dauntless air ;
The youth, still wearing on his heart
   A cherished lock of golden hair ;
The father, whose stout heart would melt
   At memories of domestic bliss ;
The boy, whose beardless cheek still felt
   The moisture of a mother's kiss.

Such was the host which Freedom sent
   To guard her temple's holy fane,
Till in our Southern land was spent
   The storm of Treason's leaden rain.

To-night we call the roll again.
  Who answers "Here?" Not all! Not all!
Where are the ranks of stalwart men,
  Who sprang to that first bugle call?

Look down the line and see to-night
  Old men whose heads are silver-crowned ;
Too blind to see the musket's sight,
  Too deaf to hear the bugle sound.
That stooping form is out of line :
  That crutch, my friend, is much too slow :
That armless sleeve, old comrade mine,
  Could never strike the charging foe.

That trembling frame could never stand
  The weary march, the tentless bed :
No foe would fly that nerveless hand,
  And fear would mock that palsied tread.
The gallant host, which, in its prime,
  Once seemed to spurn the earth they trod,
Stands shaken by the hand of Time,
  And dwindled to an "awkward squad."

Yet all these gaps along the line,
  So vacant unto other sight,
Dear comrades, to your eyes and mine,
  Are filled with shadow forms to-night.

Here some who sleep beneath the clay
   Of Southern fields stand forth again ;
Here some, who grieved their lives away,
   Shut up in Treason's prison pen.

Here from sepulchral field and wood
   They gather at the bugle call,
And stand again, as once they stood,
   In manly beauty, strong and tall,
And as we call each cherished name
   That grief has blotted with a tear,
Life seems to stir each spectral frame,
   And ghostly voices answer, "Here !"

Each year some dear, familiar face
   To Memory's keeping we consign ;
Each year some comrade takes his place
   Among the shadows in the line.
And thus the living ranks grow thin.
   Ah, few must be the years, at most,
Before we all are mustered in,
   To serve among the silent host.

But while we live, though halt and blind,
   And shattered by the storms of war,
Our country's bugle call will find
   "All present—or accounted for."

And 'neath our flag of Stripes and Stars
  We'll gather still as comrades true,
Till Freedom stoops to kiss the scars
  Of her last, dying Boy in Blue.

WHAT SHALL IT TEACH?

[Read at the laying of the corner-stone of the Soldiers' Monument, at Indianapolis, August 22, 1889.]

IF a stranger be here, and shall wonder,
    Why thus do the people convene?
Why do cannon awake with their thunder
    A land all so blessed and serene?
Why the old and the new generation,
    Like pilgrims, turn hither their tread,
And unite with the head of the Nation
        To honor our dead?

Let him ask of the age-stricken mother,
    Still mourning the loss of a son ;
Let him ask of the father or brother,
    Who saw, when the battle was done,
The brow of the loved one, where valor
    Had shone like a crown through the fray,
With the red wound of death on its pallor
        At close of the day.

Let him ask of the maimed on their crutches ;
   The heroes whose sleeves are unfilled ;
Or of thousands whose frames at the touches
   Of pain into anguish are thrilled :
And their hearts, overfilled with their yearning,
   Shall turn to our dead where they lie ;
But his eyes shall be proud in their burning,
     Who thus shall reply :—

Once before did a people assemble,
   As now, from the city and plain,
But the country's great heart was a-tremble ;
   Her bosom was red with a stain ;
For a child of her earliest nursing,
   Astray in dissension and strife,
Had mocked her affection with cursing,
     And struck at her life.

And the cannon of Treason had sounded
   Its challenge to war on the coast,
But from patriot hearts there rebounded
   An echo to answer the boast.
And the 'larum from drum and from steeple
   Called Liberty's sons to her need ;
And for this had assembled the people,
     To bid them God speed.

There were tears on the roses of beauty;
   The lips of the mothers were white;
But the frown on the stern face of Duty
   Grew black as it girded for fight;
And the land was astir with the rattle
   Of arms, and the bugles were loud,
Till southward the blaze of the battle
    Burst red through its cloud.

Then was wrought for the future a story,
   That children of ages to come
Shall read, and be stirred at its glory
   As hearts at the roll of a drum.
And over the battles and marches
   The tears of the mothers shall shine
In a rainbow that clasps in its arches
    Palmetto and pine.

For the wager of battle decided
   That over the patriot's grave
One flag of a land undivided
   Henceforth and forever shall wave.
And now have the people assembled
   To rear up a shaft to our dead,
For the country that sorrowed and trembled
    Has blessing instead.

'Tis not that the land may remember
    The red wounds of war, and its rage :—
Like ashes that lie on an ember,
    Let Time spread his dust on the page.
'Tis not that the names of our heroes
    Shall live, though the ages shall pass :—
What are Fame's Alexanders or Neroes
      But breath on a glass?

Our comrades lie wrapped in their glory—
    So let us record on the stone.
Like the night was the page of our story :
    Their blood washed it bright as the sun.
What praises can heighten the splendor
    Of those who have died for a trust?
The tears of the brave and the tender—
      Give these to their dust.

But this be our Monument's teaching—
    A tongue that shall never be dumb—
A voice through the future far-reaching,
    To tell generations to come,
How, under the plowshare of Treason,
    The lives of our heroes were sown
That the fruit might be theirs, and the season
      Of harvest their own.

That the flag which their fathers have given,
    Unsullied, untorn to their hands,
Must float in the free air of Heaven,
    Till Time shall have numbered his sands.
And to them shall the mission be granted
    To rule on the shore and the waves,
While the staff of that banner is planted
    On patriot graves.

RESPONSE.

[On behalf of Dunbar Post, G. A. R., to an address by Rev. J. P. Hutch-
inson.]

W E who were once the "Boys in Blue"—
  Though now, indeed, old men in gray—
Return our grateful thanks to you
  Who bid us welcome here to-day.
We come, the comrades of the dead,
As men through sacred chancels tread,
To share with you the holy trust
That bids us guard their hallowed dust.

We come, but not with martial stride,
  As once upon the march we pressed ;
Like stragglers now, we turn aside,
  And tarry by the way for rest.
The long campaign is almost done :
Our march is toward the setting sun ;
And soon the vale will come in sight
Where we must bivouac for the night.

What praise should greet us for the past
    We may not say.   So let it stand.
He strikes but for his own at last,
    Who battles for his native land.
And those were times when all were brave ;
The wife, the mother, as she gave
Her loved ones to her country's call,
Their toils, their wounds—she felt them all.

Oh, not upon the field of blood
    Came wounds that gave the sorest pain :
But where the white-lipped women stood,
    Whose hope, whose happiness, was slain.
For every death-shot of the fray
Had double mission ; far away
It found some heart, some bosom fair,
And made its final lodgement there.

Then for our dead ring funeral bells,
    And scatter flowers with bounteous hand ;
But crown with fadeless immortelles
    The wives, the mothers of the land.
Quick to our native land's appeal
Her sons will spring with leveled steel ;
But Freedom's surest safeguard lies
In woman's brave self-sacrifice.

You call us brave? So were our sires ;
  So are our sons ; and so must be
Each generation that aspires
  To bear the torch of Liberty.
The fire that made the winter snow
On Plymouth Rock seem summer's glow
Is burning yet, and still will burn,
While father's teach what sons should learn.

Should tread of hostile feet resound,
  And foes invade, by field or flood,
The soil, thus christened holy ground
  By woman's tears and patriot blood,
Each step would meet a Spartan band,
And some Leonidas would stand
In every pass from sea to sea,
And make a new Thermopylæ.

For us the battle storm is past ;
  Its crimson rain has washed away
The blot whose inky blackness cast
  A shadow o'er our fairest day.
Now Freedom wraps her flag of stars
About her breast to hide her scars,
And Peace, returning dove, has brought
The olive branch for which she sought.

Why should we weep for those whose camp
    Is pitched on the eternal shore,
Since Freedom guards their funeral lamp
    Upon her shrine for evermore?
The sun that set for them arose
Upon a day new-born for those
Who live to bless the God whose hand
Has poured such blessings on the land.

And we who tarry yet awhile,
    To reap fruition of our toil,
Behold the sun of promise smile
    And shed its gladness on the soil.
The guiding light which rose for them
Was Freedom's Star of Bethlehem ;
But we have lived to see and bless
Her glorious Sun of righteousness.

MISCELLANEOUS.

WAITING.

I.

THERE'S a thought I am waiting to think,
   And the world, in its rapture, shall drink
   At its fountain of wisdom and truth ;
But, somehow, 'tis marred in the shaping,
Or, burst from my grasp and escaping,
   It flies like the visions of youth.

Sometimes it will flash on my eyes,
Like the lightning's red blaze on the skies,
   Or the sun in the face of the blind :
But, somehow, it pales into glimmers,
As vague as the moon when it shimmers,
   From waters upheaved by the wind.

'Tis a thought I shall yet understand,
And a fountain shall gush in the land,
   And the world its nepenthe shall drink.
Then hearts shall be glad at the story,
And deathless shall be in its glory
   The thought I am waiting to think.

II.

There's a joy I am waiting to know,
And my heart shall drink deep of its glow,
   As a pomegranate drinks of the sun :
But, somehow, my pain ever measures
Its depth by the height of my pleasures—
   Its tears by the smiles I have won.

Sometimes I behold it appear,
And in garlanded beauty draw near,
   And 'tis bright as the glory of morn ;
But, somehow, it always must borrow
One rose from the garden of sorrow,
   And bleed with the wound of the thorn.

'Tis a joy that I yet shall possess,
To lie down in my heart, and to bless
   All my life with the warmth of its glow.
Then Hope shall be strong to endeavor,
And Faith shall go trusting forever
   The joy I am waiting to know.

III.

There's a song I am waiting to sing ;
'Tis a weird and a mystical thing,
  And I hear it sometimes in my dreams ;
But, somehow, I can not remember—
Like ice-covered brooks in December,
  Its half-uttered melody seems.

Like a lute, half bereft of its strings—
Like a window-harp, swept by the wings
  Of the wind in its languishing flight ;
But, somehow, it sinks into sighing,
As, e'en of its ecstacy dying,
  It swoons on the breast of the night.

There are times when its harmony wells,
Like the ringing of far-away bells,
  Swinging ever in rhythmical time ;
But, somehow, it drifts away, sobbing,
And only my heart, in its throbbing,
  Goes on with the echoeless chime.

Sometimes it pours over my soul,
Like the music of anthems that roll
  Through cathedral aisles, solemn and vast ;
But, somehow, the voice of the singers
Dies out, and my soul, as it lingers,
  Bows down in the silence, aghast.

Sometimes 'tis so joyous in tone
That it drowns all the piteous moan
  Of the deep diapason of woe ;
But, somehow, ambition will languish,
And hopes, that have perished in anguish,
  Lie pallid as corpses in snow.

'Tis a song that I know will be sung,
When my spirit shall find it a tongue,
  And my lute shall be given a string :
Then hearts shall be joyous to madness,
And nations shall chant, in their gladness,
  The song I am waiting to sing.

IV.

There's a deed I am waiting to do,
And the crown of the brave and the true
  I shall then proudly set on my brow :
But, somehow, it flies from me ever,
And, spite of my bravest endeavor,
  I can not accomplish it *now*.

I know there is strength in my soul,
And it ever yearns on to the goal,
  With my heart and my hope in its trust ;
But, somehow, the goal seems receding.
And souls make but pitiful speeding,
  While shod with these sandals of dust.

But *when* the great deed shall be done,
And the guerdon of labor is won,
   And my heart shall its courage renew,
Then all men, their voices upraising,
Shall never grow weary of praising
   The deed I am waiting to do.

1879.

WHAT IS LIFE?

WHAT is life, that we sigh as we measure
Its flight by the swiftness of years?
A groping for phantoms of pleasure,
  That hide in the mist of our tears;
A moment of laughter or sobbing;
  A burning of love or of lust;
A heart that is spent with its throbbing,
    And crumbles to dust.

What is hope, that we call it eternal?
  A flash on the darkness afar;
A ray from the regions supernal,
  But brief as the fall of a star.
Too swift for the feet of the mortal,
  Too slow for the wings of the soul;
A meteor seen at the portal,
    But lost at the goal.

What is love, that we yearn for its favor?
  A vintage, bright-beaded with tears;
A sweetness despoiled of its savor,
  When touched by the mildew of years;

A torture from promise of gladness ;
  A sting from the thorn of a rose ;
A blossom with fruitage of sadness,
    That robs of repose.

What is pleasure, that mocks our pursuing?
  A glow 'round the gloom of eclipse ;
A yearning as vain as the wooing
  Of kisses on pallid dead lips ;
A priestess unveiling the idol
  Where peace is in sacrifice slain ;
A skeleton decked for the bridal
    That weds us to pain.

What is death, that a handful of ashes
  Should claim from the living a sigh?
Black robes for a day, and wet lashes,
  That kisses of laughter shall dry ;
A silence, a semblance of sorrow :
  A sleeper that heedeth it not ;
A heaping of clay, and to-morrow,
    Alone and forgot.

1885.

JONATHAN SNOW.

JONATHAN SNOW was decrepit and old,
    And his poor, ragged form you had pitied to see;
Yet a king, in his mantle of purple and gold,
    Was never so cheerful and happy as he.
"My coat isn't new, but it's roomy and free;
    My hat isn't quite in the fashion, I know;
If others have better it's nothing to me;
    They may wear them, and welcome," says Jonathan
        Snow.

He lived in a poor little hovel alone,
    And you'd scarcely feel safe in its wind-shaken
        walls;
Yet a lord in his ivy-crowned castle of stone
    Was never so proud of his tapestried halls.
"Though opulence passes, and pride never calls,
    There's room, and to spare, for affection, I trow;
If others delight in their parties and balls,
    They may have them, and welcome," says Jona-
        than Snow.

His old frame was bent as he passed on his way,
    And his tottering limbs were distorted by pain;
But the rich in their chaises were never more gay
    Than he, as he stumped on his hickory cane.

"My horse hasn't quite so much mettle, 'tis plain,
  But death comes as soon to the swift as the slow ;
If others love better the whip and the rein,
  They may have them, and welcome," says Jona-
    than Snow.

His friends were the children, the poor and the old,
  And his greeting was cheerful, his smile was benign.
Not Crœsus, with all of his silver and gold,
  Could purchase a love of a purer design.
"The friendship that dwells in the sparkle of wine
  Will break with its bubbles and die with its glow ;
If others want friends that are truer than mine,
  They may have them, and welcome," says Jonathan
    Snow.

He worshiped, in faith, the great Ruler above,
  Though builders of creeds would have thought him
    remiss ;
But he taught the sweet doctrine of patience and love,
  And he found in its practice a heaven of bliss.
"There is healing in kindness ; a tear and a kiss
  Can lighten the heart that is heavy with woe.
If others want better religion than this,
  They may have it, and welcome," says Jonathan
    Snow.

One evening, Death entered his poor little hut,
　And Jonathan smiled, when he saw he was there;
For be the door open or be the door shut,
　The soul that is ready has naught to prepare.
"The seed-time was pleasant, the summer was fair,
　The harvest was garnered a long time ago;
There are only the gleanings awaiting my care;
　You may have them, and welcome," says Jonathan
　　Snow.

　1879.

THE GIRLS OF THE WEST.

O THE girls of the West! the fairest, the best!
   Go search the world over, and vain is the quest;
In the valleys below, on the mountains above,
You will find not a maiden more worthy of love.
       With footsteps as light
       As the thistle-down's flight,
       Or the moonbeams at night,
        As they fall on the snow,
       They are cheery and blithe,
       And their forms are as lithe
       As the willows that writhe
        Where the summer winds blow.
Their brows are as clear as the vaporless air;
But Cupid lies hid in the mesh of their hair,
His bow ever bent and his arrow in rest,
And the wounds have been sore in the hearts of the
    West.

O, the girls of the West! No bee ever seeks
The honey in roses more fair than their cheeks;
No humming-bird ever to drunkenness sips
A nectar so sweet as the wine of their lips.

But the rose hath a thorn
That can wound or can warn,
And the saucy lips scorn
    A false wooer's caress ;
But Love hath his due,
When he kneeleth to sue,
And the heart that is true
    They are ready to bless.
Then here's to the maiden, whose heart is as gay
As her own native birds on the wind-shaken spray ;
But, mated, what bird is so true to its nest,
Or so constant in love as the girls of the West?
1879.

THE REAPERS.

I SAW the morn, half-wakened, stand
Upon the glowing hills, and fair
The fingers of her rosy hand
Played through her wealth of golden hair;
The music of the vale was sweet
With tinkling sounds of stirring herds,
And gay woodpeckers loudly beat
The morning drum that wakes the birds.

Where sweet wild roses lined the brook
The winds were bathing in perfume;
Their wings the insect nomads shook,
And issued from their tents of bloom;
The dew hung bright on tree and plant,
And o'er the yellow harvest field
The early sunbeams fell aslant,
Like javelins on a golden shield.

Among the ranks of ripened grain,
I saw the wind-waves chasing run,
As billows sport upon the main,
And seaward roll to meet the sun;

And while the shadows still were long,
  And covered half the plain below.
Across the field, with shout and song,
  I saw the reapers come and go.

Among the harvest sheaves I stood,
  When day's last embers faintly burned,
And shadows of the gnomon wood
  Were eastward on their dial turned:
And blotted from the gleaming grain
  Was all the morning's rosy glow;
Yet still across the harvest plain
  I saw the weary reapers go.

And thus, I sighed, when man has wrought
  Through all the long and burning day,
To bind the gleaming sheaves of thought,
  Till life in twilight blends away,
He finds that shadows have concealed
  The glories of the harvest plain,
And stands, a reaper yet afield,
  Among the ripe, ungathered grain.

1878.

TO W. H. G.

I WANDERED once in a gloomy vale,
  Where the mists and the shadows 'round me
    lay,
And I felt the strength of my spirit fail,
  As I journeyed slower, day by day.
The light of the rosy morn had fled,
  And the noontide sun had lost its glow,
And the leaden shroud of the vapors spread
  O'er the twilight land where I must go.

But, as I faltered, a brave, strong hand
  Reached through the shadows and clasped my
    own,
And the mists of the valley were Iris-spanned,
  As the sun of promise among them shone.
My soul leaped up like a man unbound,
  And my laggard feet were shod with speed,
For my heart was rich with a wealth new-found
  In the priceless worth of a friend indeed.

1893.

THE AUTUMN QUEEN.

A WREATH of yellow leaves and red
    She twined about her golden hair,
And, laughing gaily, thus she said—
    For she was young, and very fair—
"Behold my crown and regal mien,
And bow before the Autumn Queen."

"Nay, nay, my dear," I made reply—
    For I am old, and thus may speak—
"Your right to reign I must deny;
    Behold! a rose on either cheek!
You but usurp the throne, I fear,
For Autumn hath no roses, dear."

Her sunny head the maiden shakes—
    "They are not roses, sir," she said,
" 'Tis but the color Autumn takes
    To paint the ripening apples red.
With younger eyes you might have seen,
And owned me still the Autumn Queen."

"You wear your crown with regal grace,
    But though the Autumn gave the red,
How came those lilies in your face,
    Since lilies with the Summer fled?
A sweet impostor, still, I fear,
Since Autumn hath no lilies, dear."

"How can you thus mistake them so?
    Such treason well deserves a frown ;
They are not lilies, but the snow
    That Autumn steals from Winter's crown.
Come, bow you, sir, with courtly mien,
And own me now the Autumn Queen."

"Nay, nay! Yet deem me not too bold!
    I grant the Autumn white and red ;
But all this flossy sheen of gold,
    In floods of glory round your head—
The warmth of Summer's glow is here,
And Autumn's gold is chill, my dear."

"I thought not age could be so dull!
    Behold! On every woodland spread,
Where Summer's chalice, grown too full,
    Was spilled along the way she fled!
And thus my hair has caught the sheen
That proves me now the Autumn Queen."

" 'Twere sweet to worship and obey ;
    And I could yield allegiance true,
But ah ! those azure eyes betray
    Too much of Summer's vanished blue.
I would not doubt—and yet—and yet,
The Autumn hath no violet."

"They are not violets.   The hue
    Which so deceives your failing eyes
Is but reflection of the blue
    Which Autumn paints along the 'skies.
And so, despite your doubts, I ween,
You now must own me Autumn Queen."

I was not all convinced, but still,
    My heart was sad to see her grieved ;
For winsome maids must have their will,
    And age is glad to be deceived.
"And yet—and yet," I could but say,
"You should have been the Queen of May."
1885.

THE DREAMER.

BESIDE his desk, in absent mien,
 He sits, his weary head alean
 Upon his idle hand ;
Idle, because his thoughts to-day
Are playing truant, far away,
 Beyond his will's command.

Unbalanced books before him lie ;
A score of letters wait reply :
 He sees, he heeds them not.
Across the page, but just begun,
The lines are at wild angles run,
 And ended with a blot.

No rush of barter through the street,
 Nor hurried tramp of eager feet,
 Upon his senses fall ;
For one low voice from out the past
Has whispered to his soul and cast
 A silence over all.

Those figured columns, reared to wealth
Above the grave of peace and health,
  No longer yield delight;
For on his brow he feels a hand
That reaches from the shadow-land
  And shuts them from his sight.

Those lips, where scorn has set its seal,
To bind the moan when sorrow's steel
  Has stabbed the heart of bliss,
Are parted with a smile of grace,
And bend above a shadow face
  That answers with a kiss.

The heart, shut in its gloomy cell,
While Mammon's sleepless sentinel
  Before the portal lay,
Has stirred within its tomb at last;
One angel, summoned from the past,
  Has rolled the stone away.

Ah, what strange influence is this
That wooes him back to youth and bliss,
  And holds his spirit there,
While, void of soul and void of mind,
The toil-worn frame remains behind,
  A shriveled husk of care?

We may not know. And why should we
Weigh with our cold philosophy
   The alchemy of bliss?
As well to tear the rose apart,
To prove, by laying bare its heart,
   From whence its sweetness is.

Oh, dreams that come on noiseless wings,
From that white-misted vale, where sings
   Ambition's dying swan!
How fair ye are! but false as fair,
To cheat the twilight hour of care
   With whisperings of the dawn!

Some rainbows of the vanished years
Will span the rainfall of our tears,
   E'en when the heart grows old;
But, vain as in our childhood's search,
We miss the fast-receding arch,
   And lose our pot of gold.

1885.

THE ROSE-TREE.

I CAN not but think there is something amiss.
   I envy no man his possessions, God knows!
But it seemeth to me there is justice in this:
   "Who owneth the rose-tree should gather the rose."

I planted a rose-tree, I watched it with care;
   I trained it up tenderly, taught it to climb;
God gave it the sunshine and gave it the air,
   And I said: "He will give me its roses in time."

My cottage was humble, my garden was small,
   But grand enough, large enough, both for my love.
The house of my neighbor was stately and tall,
   And flung me its shadow, in scorn, from above.

I nurtured my rose till at length it o'ergrew
   The poor broken wall of my garden, and clung
To the house of my neighbor; then upward it drew,
   Far above and o'erlooking the spot where it sprung.

I sighed, for I counted it wholly mine own,
   But I said: "It is strong, and ambitious to grow;
Let it cling to my neighbor's proud mansion of stone
   I will still have the roses that blossom below."

Alas, for my hope! It grew up, and grew on;
  It reached the high window, it clung to the sill;
It bloomed round the casement as red as the dawn,
  But below it is barren and blossomless still.

My neighbor has roses, a surfeit of sweet;
  They garland his board when the banquet is spread.
I have but the dead ones that fall at my feet,
  Flung down in disdain when their fragrance has fled.

I sigh as I think of the wearisome years
  I waited and watched for the fruits of my love,
But still, as I water the root with my tears,
  My neighbor is plucking the roses above.

I envy him not what has climbed to his hand;
  God's rain and God's sunshine have caused it to grow;
But still, it seems hard he has only to stand
  And pluck off the fruits of my labor below.

So it seemeth to me there is something amiss.
  And will it continue thus ever? God knows!
But right is still right, and there's justice in this:
  "Who owneth the rose-tree should gather the rose."
    1883.

TO B. S. P.

OLD friend of mine, had I the skill
    To sing the songs I often dream,
There's one—could memory but recall—
The noblest, sweetest of them all,—
    Should take thee for its theme.

Its plaintive minor-chords should tell
    How bravely patient souls may be;
Its major tones triumphant rise,
To sing the grand, the high emprise
    Of worth's humility.

And interwoven with it all,
    Like sigh of wind with songs of birds,
Should love's low melody be wrought,
With thrill of sense and wealth of thought,
    Transcending power of words.

But vain the wish; I can but reach
    My hand in silence, as I bend
In homage to thy poet art,
And offer all I have—my heart—
    To pay thy love, my friend.

1893.

THE OLD SCHOOLMASTER.

H E sat by his desk at the close of the day,
   For he felt the weight of his many years.
His form was bent and his hair was gray,
   And his eyes were dim with the falling tears.
The school was out and his task was done,
   And the house seemed now so strangely still,
As the last red beam of the setting sun
   Stole silently over the window-sill.

Stole silently into the twilight gloom;
   And the deepening shadows fell athwart
The vacant seats, and the vacant room,
   And the vacant place in the old man's heart.
For his school had been all in all to him,
   Who had wife, nor children, nor land, nor gold;
But his frame was weak and his eyes were dim,
   And the fiat was issued at last—"Too old!"

He bowed his head on his trembling hands
   A moment, as one might bend to pray:—
"Too old! they say: and the school demands
   A wiser and younger head to-day.

Too old! Too old! But these men forgot
    It was I who guided their tender years.
Their hearts were hard and they pitied not
    My trembling lips and my falling tears.

"'Too old! Too old!' It was all they said.
    I looked in their faces one by one,
But they turned away, and my heart was lead.
    Oh, God of the stricken, Thy will be done!"
The night stole on, and a blacker gloom
    Was over the vacant benches cast;
The master sat in the silent room,
    But his mind was back in the days long past.

And the shadows took, to his tear-dimmed sight,
    Dear, well-known forms, and his heart was thrilled
With a blessed sense of its old delight,
    For the vacant benches all were filled.
And he slowly rose at his desk, and took
    His well-worn Bible, that lay within,
And he said, as he lightly tapped the book:
    " It is the hour—let school begin ! "

And he smiled, as his kindly glances fell
    On the well-beloved faces there—
John, Rob, and Will, and laughing Nell,
    And blue-eyed Bess, with the golden hair,

And Tom, and Charley, and Ben, and Paul—
  Who stood at the head of the spelling class—
All in their places,—and yet they all
  Were lying under the grave-yard grass.

He read the Book, and he knelt to pray,
  And he called the classes to recite;
For the darkness all had rolled away
  From a soul that saw by an inward light.
With words of praise for a work of care,
  With kind reproof for a broken rule,
The old man tottered, now here, now there,
  Through the spectral ranks of his shadow-school.

Thus all night long, till the morning came,
  And darkness folded her robe of gloom,
And the sun looked in with his eye of flame,
  On the vacant seats of the silent room.
The wind stole over the window-sill,
  And swept through the aisles in a merry rout;—
But the face of the master was white and still:
  His work was finished, and school was out.
1878.

INDIANA.

I LOVE New England's sea-girt strand,
    Where, his Atlantic voyage o'er,
The day steps lightly to the land
    And journeys westward from the shore ;

For all her sunlit hills are fair,
    And silver-tongued are all her streams,
And joys that blessed my spirit there
    Still mingle with my sweetest dreams

And oft, when vagrant Fancy flings
    Her baubles down, as day declines,
I hear in Memory's rustling wings
    The singing of the mountain pines.

But fairer scenes and softer skies
    Await the later day's caress,
Where Indiana, smiling, lies,
    The blossom of the wilderness.

Her forests spread their arms to greet
    A rosy flood of summer air,
And plains fall languid at her feet,
    O'erburdened with the wealth they bear.

Her singing streams in gladness run
  Through vocal wood and flowery lea,
And carry southward to the sun
  The pearls he borrowed from the sea.

Triumphant march her woodmen beat
  Where Progress moves, all-conquering,
While homesteads rise about her feet,
  Like roses in the path of spring.

Till, fair as ocean billows, glide
  The waves across her harvest plain,
And sweeter than the murmuring tide,
  The rustling of the golden grain.

Oh, dearer is our lovely vale,
  With hamlets from the forest won,
Than all the pine-clad hills, where trail
  The sea-wet tresses of the sun.

Fair Indiana, may the hand
  Of Progress touch thee but to bless ;
And Peace with plenty crown the land,
  That blossomed from the wilderness.
1877.

CROOKED JIM.

THE thoughtless would laugh if you mentioned his
    name ;
  The heartless would taunt him and jeer ;
For his reason was lit by a flickering flame,
  And his body was crooked and queer.
The sport of all jokers was poor Crooked Jim,
  As he wandered, unfriended, alone ;
And Charity's self, when petitioned by him,
  Only mocked him and gave him a stone.

The brain that lay chilled in his carroty poll
  No fires of ambition could warm :
But earth has no standard to measure the soul
  That was cramped in his poor crooked form.
We measure a man by his stature, and so,
  In our blindness, we call him sublime ;
But the height of the spirit we never can know,
  Till we learn it in His good time.

   *   *   *   *   *   *   *

There is rush on the street—there is hurry, and near
  The clatter of hoofs and of wheels !
A crowd that is suddenly stricken with fear,
  Surging back to the walls as it reels !

A tempest of dust down the thoroughfare blown!
  Two horses with terror gone wild!
And clinging, white-faced, in the carriage, alone—
  God of mercy! now pity the child!

Oh, now for aid of a swift, fearless hand!
  Is there one in this fear-stricken host?
Can the sight of that pleading white face not command
  All the manhood and strength that ye boast?
Not one? Oh cravens! shrink back to the wall!
  Turn white, as ye hold in your breath!
Are the souls in your proud, stalwart bodies so small,
  That ye falter and tremble at death?

Not one? Nay, but stay! Did ye not see it bound,
  Like a dark ball, out into the street?
See! The heads of the horses sink down to the
    ground.
  What is that trailing under their feet?
Ah, haste to the rescue—the danger is o'er—
  But the mad hoofs are beating his breast.
Ye may venture there now, ye who trembled before,
  For he holds them—go finish the rest.

Strong hands that but now were all palsied with dread
  Have the little one safe in their clasp.
But poor Crooked Jim—he is lying there—dead,
  With the reins in his stiffening grasp.

There is blood on the body that late was his shame;
   There is dust in his carroty hair;
But the soul that leaped out of that poor crooked
       frame,
   Stands as high as the high heavens are.

1883.

THE OLD TRAMP.

H E came to the door at the close of the day,
    When the winds of the winter blew cold.
They saw he was ragged, decrepit and gray—
He was "only a tramp" and they turned him away,
    Nor would heed the sad story he told.

They mocked at his sorrow and bade him begone,
    Nor trouble their peace with his prayer:
And though he had traveled from earliest dawn,
He turned from the door and went tottering on,
    With a heart that was chill with despair.

For why should his sorrow intrude on their mirth,
    Like a skeleton guest at a feast?
To be poor is a sin, and the standard of worth
Is the chance that distributes the portions of earth,
    And the vilest is he who has least.

He saw through the window the ruddy light glow,
    And he turned with a sorrowful gaze
To envy the comfort denied him, when, lo!
A vision came down from the years long ago,
    Like a picture afloat in the blaze.

A picture of home that was happy as this,
　Where had waited a beautiful form
To greet his return with a smile and a kiss,
And his heart grew so full to o'erflowing with bliss,
　That he felt not the wrath of the storm.

All the wearisome tramping, the hunger, and tears,
　And the cold—they were only a dream.
All the nights without shelter, the burden of years—
He laughs at them now, as before him appears
　This light with its welcoming gleam.

Again he is young, with a heart that is brave;
　Again is a husband and sire;
And thankful to God for the mercy that gave
The wife—she has lain thirty years in the grave—
　Who is waiting him there by the fire.

How sweet to be home! for the tempest is wild,
　And the fire will be cheerful and bright.
Hark! was Argonaut e'er by such music beguiled?
'Tis the voice of his wife as she sings to their child—
　'Tis her shadow that crosses the light.

Why tarries he here in the tempest so long?
　He eagerly turns to the door—
Oh, Heaven! where now is the light and the song?
Alas! 'twas in dreaming, alone, he was strong;
　He wakes—he is feeble and poor.

All silent the voice and extinguished the lamp,
 And the happy ones gone to their rest ;
His brow with the dew of his sorrow is damp :
The night is less dark than the soul of the tramp,
 And less chill than the heart in his breast.

Alas ! for the home that was cheerful and warm !
 He dashes the tears from his sight ;
He gathers his rags to his shivering form,
And, turning his face to the pitiless storm,
 He totters away in the night.

If angels look down from some radiant sphere,
 Where they never grow feeble and old,
Will they smile on the happy ones slumbering here,
Or gaze on the tramp through a pitying tear
 For his crime of starvation and cold ?
 1877.

LET THEM GO.

NEED a body fret himself
   Over every puny woe?
Care is but a sorry elf,
   Dealing but a coward blow.
Striking hardest those who fly;
Wounding deepest those who sigh;
Mocking loudest when we cry;
   Need we shrink from such a foe?
Hopes are born, and hopes must die—
      Let them go!

Need a body dim his sight
   Weeping o'er dead pleasures?   No!
Though they fade like names we write
   Lightly on the melting snow,
Need we mourn and sigh for this?
Die for every Judas-kiss?
Pain and rapture, woe and bliss,
   In the warp of life, I trow,
Oft are woven "hit or miss"—
      Let them go!

Need a body scold and blame,
   Though the world, perchance, should show
Too much homage to a name
   All unworthy? Ay, and though
Modest merit hide her head,
Awed by puffed pretention's tread?
Cheek of brass and brain of lead
   Often win their laurels so.
Merit lives when these are dead—
      Let them go!

Need a body moan and pine,
   Dragging onward, faint and slow,
Drinking sorrow's bitter wine,
   Where contentment's waters flow?
Will to do, and soul to dare,
Head to win and heart to share—
In the black face of despair
   Labor's gauntlet these should throw;
And the threats of coward care—
      Let them go!

1879.

TOIL.

'TWAS in a visioned sleep my spirit saw
    The earth, as first at God's supreme behest
It came from chaos, fashioned by the hand
Of Nature, his artificer, whose skill
Obeys the will of Heaven's Omnipotence ;
And terror lurked along its lovely vales
In shape of savage beast, and death lay coiled,
With serpent fangs, among its fairest flowers ;
And wild magnificence dwelt in the hills,
Where gloomy caverns echoed back the roar
Of rushing torrents and great water-falls—
Of moaning forests and of battling storms ;
And grandeur sat beside the lonely shore,
Where heaved the ocean, like a mighty heart
Imprisoned in the rock-ribbed breast of earth ;
Tumultuous heaved, and beat the sounding coast,
As beats the captive on his dungeon bars,
Despairing, hopeless, lost, yet struggling still.
O, wildly beautiful was earth, and yet
Insentient in its beauty as the stone
Which takes, beneath the sculptor's skillful hand,

The human form divine, yet lacks the soul.
And soulless was the earth, and all unmeet
To glorify and yield its Maker praise,
For in creation's casket still it lay,
A priceless gem, yet all uncut, unset
Among the jewels in the crown of God.

   *   *   *   *   *   *   *   *

I saw a mighty spirit tread the earth,
Strong-limbed and brown, and from his ruddy brow
Great drops of sweat ran trickling down and fell
Upon the earth, and, where they lay, sprang up
The yellow harvest like a sea of gold.
He trod in majesty along the vales,
And, where his footsteps pressed the fruitful ground,
Long ranks of maize upreared their tasseled heads,
And waved green banners o'er the conquered soil.
He laid his hand upon the tangled wild—
It opened like a curtain at his touch,
And vanished like the mist before the sun.
And lo! a fruitful land, thick-studded o'er
With teeming farms, and hamlets, cities, towns,
Whence rose the songs of joyous industry—
The sweetest sounds that reach the ears of Heaven.
He chained the heedless torrent of the hills,
Obedient to the skillful hand of thrift;
The earth he girdled with a zone of steel,

And bound the souls of water and of fire,
Subservient to his will to conquer both,
And sent them forth as messengers for man.
Where'er he trod the earth took shapelier form,
And generous-handed Plenty followed close.
Brown Agriculture bared his dewy brow,
To do him grateful homage as he passed;
While fair Pomona spread her wealth of fruit,
And Ceres piled her sheaves of golden grain,
And queenly Commerce dipped her pennon low,
To greet the conqueror of land and sea.
And then I heard resound through all the land
One mighty voice of song and grateful praise,
And earth held up her thankful hands to Heaven,
And blessed her Maker for the gift of Toil.

1880.

THE MORNING AND THE EVENING STAR.

ERE Dawn had put her curtains by,
    And set her golden gates ajar,
Suspended in the eastern sky
    I saw a brightly-beaming star.
"O, harbinger of day !" I cried,
    "Thy soft, benignant light shall be,
Through all my life, whate'er betide,
    A star of peace and hope to me."

And often ere the night had fled,
    To see its glorious light I came,
Before the morn awoke to tread
    Her upward path of crimson flame.
And though amid the brighter glare
    It seemed to fade and die away,
I knew that still it lingered there,
    A star of hope through all the day.

Till once, I found, when youth was gone,
    That pleasure lured but to deceive :
Then Hope, that entered with the dawn,
    Fled westward to the gates of eve.

My soul sank down in dark despair,
  Till lo! a radiant light afar!
And then I knew that Hope was there,
  The softly-beaming Evening Star.

And now, when night with dusky hands
  Has closed the gates behind the day,
Still like a beacon-light it stands
  To cheer my spirit with its ray.
And looking through the gloom afar
  I see a land of peace and rest,
And find in that calm Evening Star
  Life's latest promise and its best.

1879.